Praise Jc

"I think I've just read the best book I'm likely to read in 2015. *Godbomb!* is that good. No, not just good. It's great."

- Cemetery Dance

"This horror/thriller/drama is written in a style both beautifully thought-provoking and breathlessly immediate, and my jealousy for the author's talent almost makes me hate him for it."

- Jonathan Butcher, Splatterpunk Award-nominated author of Something Very Wrong

"It's vulnerable, authentic and universal. Any reader could find themselves in this situation. Gripping and emotional."

- Sadie Hartmann, a.k.a. Mother Horror

What do you call a one-pound note with an enormous "S" drawn on it? Read on to find out, dear friend.

A giant S-quid, of course.

Millionaires Day

Kit Power

Glossary

(Super English to Regular English)

Alsatian – German Shepherd

bent – crooked, corrupt

bonnet – of a car, the hood

boot – of a car, the trunk

building society – credit union

cane – here, to spend

carriageway – multi-lane highway

central reservation – median of a highway

dob – tattle

elasticated – elastic

estate – here, a housing development

excluded – here, permanently expelled from school

fag – cigarette

flat – apartment

gaf – apartment

gambler – slot machine

governor – here, a warden (as of a prison)

job – as a verb, to swindle

jumper – sweater

kip – nap

knickers – panties

lift – as a noun, elevator

lock-in – the practice of letting some customers stay in a bar after hours

lockup – here, a long-term storage unit

maths – math

MK3 – the postal code for Bletchley, used here akin to "90210" as shorthand for Beverly Hills

MOT certificate – Ministry of Transport certificate, akin to a state vehicle inspection certificate

muck in – pitch in

muzzy – confused, foggy

on the latch – of a door, to leave unlocked

Perspex – a brand name for hard transparent plastic, comparable to Plexiglass

pink newspaper – certain financial newspapers in the UK are printed on pink paper

poky – here, cramped or small

quid – a British pound, comparable to "buck"

redways – a system of walking and biking paths specific to Milton Keynes

rinse – here, to complete absolutely

rozzer – police officer

RTA – Road Traffic Accident

run blues – to drive with the emergency lights on, as of a police car

shufti – glance

slapper – slut

Special – here, refers to a volunteer, part-time police officer in the UK, somewhat comparable to a US military reservist

sunnies – sunglasses

the piles – hemorrhoids

towpath – a walkway beside a canal, as for towing a barge by land

treacle – here, molasses

WC – "Water Closet," meaning a bathroom

white van delivery – commercial delivery but not a professional courier, i.e. a local florist

whitey – nausea after marijuana use

wizz – methamphetamines

windscreen – here, windshield

Zafira – a brand of car

8:04 am

At 8:04 am, on Sunday 22nd December 2019, Henry Jones, unemployed and homeless, a tent-dweller in the underpass between Milton Keynes Xscape building and the shopping centre, became the first person in the United Kingdom of Great Britain and Northern Ireland to be awoken by the phenomenon that came to be known as Millionaires Day.

He was jolted from a pleasant dream of running happily with his childhood pet dog through a wood by a sudden pain in his lower back. He initially shifted his weight, trying to chase the dream back down, but the movement caused a fresh stab of discomfort, driving him to consciousness.

He opened his eyes.

The dawn light cast through the canvas roof of his tent over his belongings - the heap of blankets he was huddled under, the pile of carrier bags in the far corner - lending them a bluish tinge. He sat up, pressing his hand into the small of his back and wincing. He'd gotten used to the concrete under his thin sleeping bag over the last few weeks, but the sudden tenderness of his spine felt almost like a blow. Had there been a stone or something there? He reached behind himself, intending to run his hand over the ground to see if he could find the source of his pain…

His hand found…something. Something substantial, solid.

"The fuck?"

Henry sat up; fully awake now, his heart beating faster. He turned around, gaze moving down the sleeping bag held tight to his back, onto the shape under the canvas.

It was oblong, and judging by the raised shape it made under the groundsheet around three feet long, maybe a foot thick. Maybe thicker. Henry stared at the shape, frowning. After a few seconds, he reached out with a not quite steady hand (*it's bloody cold, of course you're shaking* he thought reflexively, but it wasn't *that* cold here in the tent and the sleeping bag, not with all the layers he was wearing) and gingerly placed it on the shape.

It felt firm.

He pushed experimentally. There was a small amount of give, but not much. The whatever-it-was had a sturdy quality. No mere cardboard box, for sure. Henry withdrew his hand and frowned some more.

"What the actual fuck?"

Kit Power

Emma Jacobs, of the Peartree Bridge estate, Milton Keynes, woke up three seconds after Henry. She'd been asleep in the back seat of her mum's car, and her small-for-a-nine-year-old frame was such that the entirety of her curled-up body lay atop the object. She'd been dreaming she was lost in a snowstorm, calling for her mother, who she knew was out in the cold with her, but whichever direction she walked, her mother's voice became fainter and fainter. She'd been rocking back and forth in her sleep, the hazy dawn light translating into her sleeping brain as the snow intensified in brightness, and her movement, coupled with the sudden appearance of the object, caused her to roll off the back seat and into the footwells.

She shivered as she opened her eyes. Her mind was still catching up to the sensation of falling, and the collision of her body with the floor. She lay still for a second, wondering if the pain was going to spike, if she'd really hurt herself in the tumble, but after a few seconds passed, and the small ache in her head and knee didn't increase dramatically, she let out a held breath (enjoying how it looked like smoke in the cold air) and allowed her mind to relax. She didn't mind sleeping out in the car during the summer, when it was warm, but in the winter, when Mum and Daddy Derek wanted private time, it often took her hours of shivering before sleep; and her dreams were bad, and she always woke with the sunrise, the light hurting her tired eyes without warming her cold skin at all, which felt like a mean joke.

She stared up at the ceiling of the car, her mind sluggishly wondering why she'd tipped off the back seat in the first place. It was slanted away from the drop, and normally if she rolled it was towards the seat backs, trying to warm herself against them...

Then she saw the handle of the case.

It was black, and seemed almost to gleam in the dawn light - as though it were wet.

Her breath caught in her throat.

Seconds after Emma was tipped from the back seat of the car she slept in, Pete Harding, of Melrose Tower, Milton Keynes, awoke in a similar manner; rolling from the edge of the mattress he'd passed out on four hours ago and landing face down on the floor. This on its own might not have been enough to wake him, given his intoxicated state, but in the process of falling, his left hand landed in the bucket of cold water that had served him so well as a bong component earlier that morning. The effect of the immersion of his hand in cold water was to cause his bladder to let go, and it was the sensation of warmth spreading around his midsection, coupled with the assault of the cold on the rest of his exposed skin, that drove him to consciousness.

The sheet nailed over the window was a poor barrier against the dawn light. Pete sat up and looked down at himself, watching the stream of urine from his limp penis slow to a trickle, then stop, mind still muzzy enough to enjoy the sensation of warm fluid over his lower stomach. He took his hand from the bong bucket and held it up in front of his eyes, before wiping it on the thin carpet to try and dry it.

Well, fuck, he thought to himself, *A New Low.* It wasn't, really - he'd shat himself in bed a couple of months ago after a spectacular two-day bender, and Rachel had given him grief about it the next day (until he'd made it clear she needed to shut the fuck up for real) but he'd just woken up with a hand soaked in stale bong water, piss all over his carpet and a pain behind his eyes that had built in the few seconds he'd opened them from a vague almost-itch to something considerably more stabby, and under those circumstances, he felt a certain amount of self-pity was not just understandable but fucking *appropriate,* and why exactly the fuck was he lying on the floor anyway, had Rachel pushed him out of bed as a funny fucking joke? He turned his head towards the mattress on the floor, and two facts slammed into his mind in quick succession.

Fact one was that it *wasn't* Rachel in his bed, but that crazy bitch Amy, which was bad for a list of reasons extensive enough that the substantial risk of having contracted an STD wasn't even in the top five. But fact two, which collided into fact one with such force that it pushed it entirely from Pete's still-stoned mind, was that there was what looked like a suitcase underneath the mattress that he had, until recently, been quite happily embracing oblivion on.

What in the actual fucking fuck?

Henry stared at the case, wondering.

It was one of those trolley suitcases with a handle and wheels. The kind he saw people pulling in and out of the train station when he'd sit down there (not exactly begging, you didn't need to beg if you picked a good spot and just sat there with a sleeping bag, people'd give you money, food, all sorts).

It looked brand new to Henry; no tags, either name or price or labels, but undamaged, pristine. Henry realised he couldn't remember the last time he'd seen something of his that looked so clean.

Something of his?

He looked around at the thought, feeling a sudden wave of guilt, as powerful as it was irrational.

Why not his?

As he stared at the polished black of hard plastic casing (*gleaming,* his still-waking mind insisted, *it's fucking gleaming*), a shadowed, distorted version of his own thin face looked back at him. Hungry. Guilty.

Couldn't be his. Too nice, too clean, too…

But it was. It fucking *was* his, under *his* tent, under *his* sleeping bag, and how it got there he didn't know but it looked new, it looked *expensive,* and…

"Fuck it," he whispered under his breath, and heaved the case upright, puffing with effort. The bastard thing was heavy, like it was full of something, and Henry felt his heart rate kick up a couple of gears, partly because of the unexpected exertion this early, sure, but partly because of something else, something he refused to name or examine, something that made him feel dizzy and sick all at once.

Despite the wheels, he lifted the case using the handles on the front and side, and, panting from the effort, carried it around to the front of his tent before placing it inside. He practically dived in after it, hand moving from trembling to shaking as he zipped the tent closed as fast as he could. Then he slowly laid the case flat on its back, looking down at that black surface, so polished it was almost fluid.

"Well, okay," he said.

Emma wasn't sure how long she'd been staring at the case. Something about the shiny blackness she could see her face in was fascinating, entrancing. She leaned forward until her breath caused the reflective surface to fog, observing that it cleared almost at once, returning to reflection.

She thought it might be a present.

She wasn't sure. It could be a trick, or a joke, but she didn't think so. Only Mum had the car keys, that was the thing. Emma supposed Daddy Derek could have gotten them, but Emma simply couldn't conceive of the man *caring* enough, even for a prank.

Her mum either, as she thought more. She tried to picture Mum opening the car, putting the case in, lifting Emma's sleeping form on top, then closing the car door quietly enough that she didn't wake, and her nose wrinkled in amused disbelief. On impulse, she grabbed and pulled the passenger side door handle.

Locked.

"No way", she said.

She looked back at the case. *A present*, her mind insisted. Had to be. From Santa? She'd not believed in him since her fifth Christmas (no presents under the tree in the shelter, not with her name on, they'd lied but she'd known), but she felt a warming surge of blood to her face at the thought. Of course, it was a couple of days early, but still... It came from somewhere. Nothing else made sense.

She felt afraid, but also excited, as she reached for the zipper.

Pete looked back at Amy lying on his side of the mattress, now, her milk-pale back still rising and falling as she slept the righteous slumber of the incurably stoned and insane. Despite his situation, he felt his cock stirring against his piss-soaked pubes. Maddeningly disjointed images flitted through his mind; her lips around a bottle top as she took a hit from the bong, her breast in his hand, nipple firm under the fabric of her T-shirt, her throaty chuckle, her looking up at him, her hips appearing above the top of her tracksuit bottoms…the images danced away again, and he exhaled, shakily. He gritted his teeth as frustration welled up. Bad enough he'd fucked himself by fucking her, but to not even have the pleasure of the memory?

Fuck it. Fuck all of it. He turned his attention back to the suitcase. He knew he wasn't dreaming, the aroma of ammonia from his nether regions settled that question, so whatever this was, it was really happening.

Wiping his still-damp hand on the thin carpet once more, as if for luck, he unzipped the case and flipped open the lid.

His eyes widened. His breath caught. His heart was suddenly pounding so hard he could feel it in his face, behind his eyes, like a fist punching out from the inside, painful. His breath left him in a grunt loud enough to make Amy stir before sinking back into oblivion, though Pete was too profoundly shocked to register the movement. He was dimly aware of his scrotum shrivelling up into a tight ball.

It can't be real. It can't be real. It can't be real.

He reached his hand out, noting with no surprise that it was shaking badly, as though the temperature in the room had plummeted, which was strange, because Pete suddenly felt uncomfortably hot, sweat appearing like a film all over his face and chest. *Pulling a whitey,* he thought, distractedly, and then his eyes moved back from his hand to the contents of the case, and his mind went back to *it can't be real, it can't be real,* as his hand reached out, *it can't be real...*

But it was.

Henry felt his mouth turn dry. He stared into the case, and the contents stared back at him - what felt like thousands of painted eyes, from a face he'd seen all his life, reproduced over and over and over in purple.

"It can't be real."

He picked up one of the bundles, calmly. There was no label on the paper band that held it in place, so he used his thumb at the corner, gently flipping the pristine sheets of paper as he counted. The bundle was tightly bound, and his fingers felt like sausages, but his mind kept it slow and steady, and as the slowness calmed his hands, he allowed the rhythm of the count to soothe him, and when his mind calmly reported a total of a hundred, he nodded to himself, believing it to be right.

So, that'd be two grand.

He picked up a second bundle, observing the way the stack bent slightly in the middle, the sheer weight of the notes causing a bowing effect. He held it up against the one he'd counted. His eyes weren't perfect, but he'd be fucked if it didn't look identical.

He looked back down at the case.

How many bundles?

Too many to count.

The tremble returned to his hands. The bundles he held fluttered, and the sound of the paper gently slapping together sounded to Henry like waves on a far-off shore.

Emma just stared. It was more money than she'd ever seen in her life. More money than she'd suspected could even *exist.*

"It must be a thousand. Maybe two thousand. Maybe *ten thousand!*"

Emma thought about her life to this point. She thought about her mother, how tightly she sometimes held Emma, how insistent she was to be on guard against The Men

Who Wanted to Take Emma Away, and she thought about the shelter, and the bed and breakfast they'd been in for what felt like forever. She thought about school, and the other children who were friendly but not her friends. She thought about Daddy Derek, who she knew wasn't her real dad (and the question she knew *never* to ask, about who her real dad was) how he looked at her like she wasn't even there, and how whenever he stayed over she slept in the car. She thought about her mum, making her promise to be a good girl, locking her in after saying good night.

She looked at the gigantic pile of money in the case on the backseat of the car, and she thought about what her mother might do when she came out to open the car and let her out.

And then, Emma burst into tears.

Pete looked over at Amy, suddenly aware that he had no idea how long he'd been staring at the enormous pile of cash neatly stacked in the case, like the world's most thoughtfully packaged bank heist score. She was still sleeping, but that wasn't what drew his attention.

What drew his attention was the suspiciously large bulge on *her* side of the mattress; the bulge that, he supposed, had caused her to roll into the middle of the bed in the first place.

A bulge that looked remarkably suitcase-sized.

Holy fucking shit.

Pete's mouth began to water.

Hour 1

8:10 am – 9:00 am

8:10 am

Henry's hands were trembling again as he pushed one of the bundles into each trouser pocket, and he made no further attempt to persuade himself it was because of the cold. He had no idea what was happening, but his months on the street had honed certain instincts, and those instincts were screaming at him to get the fuck out of here, right fucking now. He fully intended to obey them.

Cash for spending in his pockets, he lifted the case out of his tent and carried it out from under the bridge, muscles straining with the weight, executing a hilariously awkward shuffling gait. He was pretty sure Larry (next tent over) had scored smack last night, and therefore by rights should sleep through anything; on the other hand, this felt like a circumstance where an abundance of caution was not merely desirable, but essential.

So, he wrestled the case out into the grey fog of the solstice dawn before placing it on its wheels, extending the handle, and pulling it along beside him. He was trying to stay calm, but it seemed his body had other ideas, sending him a sweat to go with the shakes, and a compulsion to look in every single direction at once. *Come on, mate, it's a five minute walk to the train station, you can do this,* he thought, wishing the rumbling of the wheels on the paved walkway wasn't quite so epically fucking loud, like it was broadcasting its existence, and the incongruity of its current possessor, to everyone in a five fucking mile radius.

He tried to think ahead, work out where he was going. The train station, obviously, but then? As he trudged through the gloom, grateful that the fog was providing some visual cover, his mind ran over possible destinations. London? Bristol? Glasgow? The urge to leave, to find somewhere *away,* was incredibly powerful, fuelled by a terror at the thought that someone would come looking for the case, and what they'd do if they found him gone with it. Crazy. Why would they leave it there in the first place? But it wasn't the kind of money that someone didn't come back for, and it *was* the kind of money people went looking for.

London, that was the ticket, Henry thought. First, a clothes shop, get clean threads, then a public swimming pool, shower for about a week…no, that was no good, couldn't leave the case. Would clean clothes be enough to get a hotel room? Shit, would he need ID or a credit card for check in? Henry thought back to when he'd had a job, two-day training at head office in Birmingham - had he needed ID for the room? His passport was long gone, sold after two days of begging with no success, hunger eating at him. Never got a driving licence - other people in MK laughed at that, but Henry had always made do with a bicycle and the redways. Better for the environment. And cheaper.

Well, fuck it, some hotel would take cash, surely? As long as there was a safe in the room, he was golden. *Then* he could shower for a week, and then…?

He felt panic start to crowd in, waves of fear making him sweat even more, skin damp with it now, even as the fog chilled his face. *Then, whatever the fuck I want,* he thought angrily, teeth clenched as he pulled the case down the pavement.

8:15 am

Emma continued staring into the case, her tears drying on her cheeks as she looked at the money and thought and thought.

She thought about her mother, and how she was ill so often, how she needed her medicine. How she couldn't afford it all the time, how that made her feel, but also how she was when she *could* afford it. And Daddy Derek, how he'd always show up when one of them had money, meaning Emma would be sleeping in the car.

Emma thought that her mum finding the money would be Bad.

She couldn't articulate why, but the feeling was definite, and had only grown in the five minutes since she'd first opened the case and burst into tears.

What she didn't know was what she could do about it.

The case was too big, that was the thing. The case was too big, the car was too small. She couldn't leave the car.

Sure you could.

The thought terrified her. It was the voice of Rachel,

from her favourite TV show, about the schoolgirl who ran a hairdresser's all by herself. Emma was fuzzy on the details, but Rachel owned the place, had no parents, and worked there instead of going to school (therefore living, in Emma's personal opinion, a Perfect Life). Rachel was also sassy as *heck,* to the point where Emma's mum frequently threatened to ban Emma from watching the show, because it was A Bad Influence. The threats never came to anything, and Emma pretty much laughed them off inside, but she'd pretend to be scared sometimes, just to make life easier.

So, this wasn't the first time she'd heard Rachel's voice in her head, in that sassy, cool accent, saying something Emma herself could or should not. They'd talked often.

But this was different.

Sure, you can.

I can't. Mum's injunctions on the subject had been fierce. "The only way you stay safe is to keep this door locked. If you open it, even once, terrible things could happen. You could be taken. There are Bad Men, and they take children. Do you understand? They'd take you, and hurt you, and kill you. This. Stays. Locked." The same speech, every time she was led out to the car, and Emma felt the familiar knot of fear in her stomach as she recalled it. "You won't see them coming, they could be watching you anytime, it is *never* safe, nderstand? You're safe as long as it stays locked; if they come, you sound the horn and I'll come running, okay?"

Emma stared at the money, tears threatening again. *I can't.*

Sure, you can.

She *could*. She'd worked out how; the back doors were child locked, but the driver and front passenger doors were just...locked, and she knew how to unlock them from the inside. She could...

It felt to Emma like her hands were moving of their own accord. They took bundles of cash, two, three, four, and slid them into the elasticated waistband of her pyjamas, tucking her top back in afterwards, reaching inside to tuck the bottom of it underneath them, keeping them hidden and stopping them from slipping down her trousers. Then they zipped the case shut.

Emma stared at her own reflection in the surface of the enormous case. She'd never be able to lift it. But of course she didn't have to; as long as she could slide it off the back seat, onto the wheels, she could roll it wherever she needed to.

She looked up and down the street. The thick fog hid the canal across the road from view. There was no traffic.

She looked back toward the front seats. At the gap between them. At the driver's side door.

Was she *really* going to do this?

Apparently, she was.

She stood with one foot either side of the central divide, then moved her right leg around and through the gap between the two front seats, before swivelling her hips to place her foot down on the passenger seat. It was a stretch, and the angle was awkward, and she hopped in place, shifting her weight onto her overextended right foot. She tried to swing her other leg around, leaning forward in the process, but her heel caught the side of the chair, and she fell forward, her cheek striking the steering wheel.

The blare of the horn inside the car was deafening.

8:20 am

Pete was standing at the door to his flat. In the ten minutes since he'd woken up, he'd gone to the bathroom, using a sink full of cold water (the hot pipes made so much fucking noise, and he couldn't risk waking Crazy Amy) and the least dirty towel he owned to attempt to clean himself. Once he no longer stank of his own piss, he dressed quickly, wincing at the muted clanking of his belt buckle as he pulled up his jeans.

He then returned to the living room and looked down at the mattress on the floor. She lay on his side of the bed, curled on her side in the space he'd vacated, her hand covering her eyes, the top of her breast just visible above the sheet as it rose and fell.

He took in her dark hair, that baby face that in sleep looked positively angelic, even with the smeared black lipstick, and the milk-white skin of her shoulder. He shook his head. He'd actually fucked Crazy Amy - subject of God knew how many of his spank fantasies over the years, but comprehensively verboten for a multitude of reasons. And try as he might, he couldn't remember a single concrete thing.

That was, in Pete's humble opinion, some fucking bullshit.

Then he looked over at her side of the mattress, and the huge lump under it.

It took him several agonising minutes to get the case out from under her side, and his arms were wobbly with the strain of lifting the weight so as not to make a noise. As he did so, he rehearsed the rationale in his mind (*she's fucking crazy, she'd cane it all on drugs, probably kill herself, or someone'd job her to get it, she'd never be able to keep it secret, it's for the best*), until, by the time he'd gotten it out and upright on the floor next to his, his tired, still-stoned mind had half convinced him he *was* the good guy.

He booked a cab to Heathrow via the local cab firm's app, smiling as he tapped the 'cash' payment option. The app indicated 15 minutes. He'd wrestled with waiting inside until it arrived, but the bastard was, if the lifts were out there was no way he'd be getting the two cases down the nine flights of stairs before the cabbie had decided it was a hoax and fucked off. So he was better off taking the cases down now and waiting at the curb, though the idea made his gut churn anxiously. Still, the view from the window showed a fog so thick he couldn't even see the ground, so it'd be fine. Probably, it'd be fine.

And now he stood at the front door, two cases against the wall, checking for the fourth time that he had his passport in his backpack, the three hundred quid in twenties in his wallet - the most cash he'd ever had in his wallet at once, as he thought about it. The realisation brought on another wave of sweats.

He looked behind him, at the door that separated the narrow kitchen area he was in from the living room where Amy slept the sleep of the cataclysmically stoned. He felt a sudden powerful urge to go back in, wake her up, show her the money, then tip it all out on the mattress and screw her silly. He had a feeling she'd go for it. In fact, he was positive she would. It would be, he was quite sure, the best fuck of his life.

He closed his eyes, took a deep breath. *There's pushing your luck, and there's abusing the privilege.* Sure, it'd be quite the moment - but all the moments after it would be awful. No, time to hit the fucking road. Past time. There would be other opportunities for a young man with two mil in cash and no ties. That made him think of Rachel, and the guilt was unexpectedly powerful. But fuck it, he'd text her once he was over city lines, tell her to look under her bed. A million buys a lot of tissues. She'd get over him and his bullshit pretty quickly.

The thought made him chuckle out loud, quietly, and the sound made him jump. He straightened up and opened the door.

"Well, fuck me, that's never happened before!"

Pete's heart lurched in his chest, sending a rush of blood to his head so intense he thought it might explode.

Mental Mickey was standing on his doorstep.

He was wearing his standard uniform - black leisure suit, jacket unzipped over a plain white wife beater - Mental Mickey was a man who didn't acknowledge such petty concerns as the vagaries of the weather when it came to his wardrobe choices. The gold chain around his neck was present and correct, as was the gap-toothed grin that never seemed to falter, regardless of Mental Mickey's actual mood. There was also a bruise on his forehead that looked fresh.

There were so many reasons Mental Mickey appearing on his doorstep was spectacularly bad news that Pete felt strangely calm. It was as though the many, many reasons he was now totally and utterly fucked were too busy fighting with each other to figure out which was the most pressing, so the expected paralysing terror didn't materialise, which meant Pete was able to produce a surprisingly nonchalant "What's up, Mickey? Bit early, innit?"

He owed Mickey money. And a payment was due today. But Mickey, generally speaking, didn't make house calls, because he didn't need to. If you owed Mental Mickey money, you went to *him,* on the agreed day, at the agreed time, and you paid him what you owed, or what you'd agreed to pay in lieu of what you owed. Should you fail to make an appearance, you'd get a visit, all right, but it'd be one of the lads, not Mickey. At least, you'd hope not Mickey.

Because if Mental Mickey showed up at your door, that was Bad News.

"I'm a businessman, Pete. Money never sleeps. You'd know that if you weren't such a ganja addict."

Pete nodded, as though Mickey's own ganja habit wasn't the stuff of legend, eclipsed only by his apparently endlessly escalating appetite for amphetamines. Many was the night Pete had watched Mickey do yet another fucking line while the music pounded loud enough to wake up half the tower, thinking that this *had* to be the moment Mickey's heart finally just gave out, blew a permanent gasket from the endless speeding. Still, when Mickey was serving up shit, you ate it and smiled and asked for more.

"Yeah, okay, well, I was gonna come see you…"

Mickey's grin stayed exactly where it was, but something about it changed, and his eyes narrowed. Pete felt his stomach drop.

"You *weren't* coming to see me?"

"No, man, I said I *was* gonna come, I was…"

"I know what you said. I heard what you fucking said, didn't I? But why would you say that? Why say it, if you're gonna? Unless you weren't gonna?"

This was another reason having Mental Mickey on your doorstep was spectacularly bad news, Pete thought; the fact that the man could pick a fight in an empty room. Which would be bad enough if he wasn't also prone to sudden explosions of extreme violence with little to no warning, his five-foot six stature and loose clothes disguising a frame that was ninety eight percent muscle.

The worst part was that the instinct to grovel, while understandably strong, also had to be resisted. Pete had seen, more than once, how it went for people who showed significant weakness to Mental Mickey, and Pete preferred a life where he could chew his own food. So he went with "Fuck's sake, Mickey, I've got your cash…" as he reached for his wallet.

It was a pretty desperate semi-bluff, but Pete committed to the gesture with conviction. The trouble was, if he opened his wallet, and Mickey saw three hundred quid in place of the forty quid he was expecting, not only would Mickey take the lot as down payment against the principal, he'd also start interrogating Pete about where he'd gotten three hundred fucking quid from, and *that* was not a conversation Pete wanted to have, for approximately two million very good reasons.

Mickey caught Pete's arm. His grip was borderline painful, and trapped Pete's hand in his pocket.

"Do I look like a cunt to you? I know you've got my money, Pete."

He knows. He knows about the cases.

Pete felt the reality of it sink in. He was eye-of-the-storm calm enough to note a bitter taste in the back of his throat as his stomach clenched. *He knows. I'm fucked.* The thought landed flat and calm.

"My question for you, Pete, is where did the second bag come from?"

Pete looked over his shoulder, at the two black suitcases leaning against the wall where he'd left them. He was just turning back to face Mickey when the slap hit him, hard enough to make his eyes water.

"I asked you a fucking question."

And all at once, Pete realised this, right here, was the most compelling and immediate reason he was well and truly fucked, beyond all hope of redemption.

Because of Crazy Amy.

Mental Mickey's sister.

It was Fat Freddy that Pete's mind went to at that moment, as he stared into the face of Mental Mickey and willed his brain to unfreeze, for his mouth to say something, for fuck's sake, come out with some lie. Fat Freddy, who'd gone to school with Mickey and Amy - the one for kids who got excluded. Fat Freddy, who still lived in the tower with his mum. Fat Freddy, who'd been part of Mickey's crew from the very beginning, until New Years Eve 2015, when he'd gotten off with Crazy Amy at the big party and Mental Mickey threw him over the fourth-floor balcony.

Fat Freddy and his motor scooter, slurred speech, and colostomy bag, always smelling faintly of piss, shit, and disinfectant.

"Amy can fuck whoever she wants," Mickey would often say, "but fam are off limits to crew". It made no goddamn sense to Pete, and it didn't stop Amy flirting with anything with a cock, but Fat Freddy served as a pretty potent reminder of the consequences of a breach of policy; and as far as Pete knew, an entirely successful one.

Until, evidently, last night.

"I've got someone with me."

This time the slap was hard enough to knock him back a step. His cheek burned with the impact.

"I'm not a fucking twat, stop wasting my time. Who? Rachel?"

"No…"

"Nah, because you're not a big enough fucking idiot to run out on her, are you? So, who?"

"Some slapper I picked up last night." The sheer audacity of the obfuscation astonished Pete so much that it came out smooth and calm, even with the edge in his voice the pain had caused.

Mickey shook his head. "Well, I am fucking disappointed. And you're running out?"

Pete knew better than to argue. He settled for a shrug.

Mickey held eye contact for what felt to Pete to be a million years. Then he said, "We'll have words about this. Later. For now, round up the fucking crew. My flat, ten minutes. Tell them to bring their cases."

"What's going on, Mickey?"

"What's going on, Pete, is that, apparently, there's a black suitcase under every single bed in this block, with a million quid in each one."

"Yeah, but, I mean…"

"…and we're gonna have every single one of them. You got it?"

By we, you mean you, Pete thought with dismay. He felt his dream of escape turning into smoke, becoming one with the fog that drifted around the building. *Bring all the cases. Fuck.*

"Yeah, I got it."

"Good. Knock up Clive, Freddy, and Jim - I've tried belling them, but you know what they're like with mornings. Rich and Dave are already on the ground floor, in case anyone else gets it into their heads to do a runner. I'll get the rest. Ten minutes."

"Sure."

"Pete?"

Mickey held out his hands. Pete went back into the room, pulled up the case handles, and wheeled them over to him. Mickey nodded.

"Let the slapper sleep it off. It'll only get in the way."

You're not wrong there, thought Pete, as he followed Mickey out of the flat, closing the door quietly behind him.

8:25 am

Emma dressed as quickly as she could, trying to slow her breathing.

It was a struggle.

She looked at her pillow. In her mind, she could see the bundles of money underneath, so clearly she felt sure they must give themselves away; her mum would take one look at the bed and see the shape they made and grab them, turning on Emma, asking questions she couldn't answer.

Emma remembered the frantic rush, once she'd accidentally hit the car horn; dragging the case out of the car, arms aching with the effort, how she'd smashed her big toe when it finally fell from the seat, causing her to yelp with pain. Pulling the case around the back of the car, then shoving it as hard as she could, down her front drive and across the street, looking long enough to make sure it was swallowed by the fog. Limping back to the car, slamming and locking the door just in time. Hearing her front door open, the frantic slapping of her mother's bare feet as she ran to the car.

Lucky.

Lucky she'd been crying because of the pain in her

foot. Lucky she'd locked the door, gotten rid of the case. Saying she'd seen someone in the fog, pain giving her voice an edge that sounded like fear (and of course there *was* fear - fear of being caught in a lie, fear of Mum finding the money she'd hidden in the waistband of her pyjama trousers).

Mum had been cross, of course, but the tears had calmed her down, and when Daddy Derek started shouting about being woken up by the bloody car horn, Mum had yelled at him to shut the eff up, and he had.

And now she was dressing in her room, thinking about the money and how she absolutely could *not* do what she was thinking of doing; *could not* finish getting dressed, take the money from under her pillow and walk into the city centre. To Claire's. To Build-A-Bear. To ToyZ N GamZ.

She could not.

Sure, you can.

Emma was inside the salon, as she often was in her imagination, especially when things were difficult at home, Mum angry or sad, arguing with Daddy Derek or just curled up on the sofa, tired and unhappy; Emma would hang out with Rachel, learning how to cut hair, clean up the shop, and just being super sassy together. Like sisters. She knew it was make-believe - she was nine, for cripes sakes, not a *baby* - but that didn't make it any less comforting; being able, sometimes, to go into a world that felt safe, that made sense, and where she had a friend.

Only this time, Rachel wasn't just playing or reciting jokes from the show; this time, Rachel was telling her she could do something she knew was wrong.

It was morning, so the salon hadn't opened yet. Rachel was looking at her, hand on hip, that smile Emma just loved playing on her lips, the one that said delightful shenanigans were basically guaranteed. Except what she was saying was, "Sure, you can. Your mom (Emma loved how Rachel said the word, her accent) has gone back to bed. Daddy Derek is here, and there's no school. She told you to make your own breakfast, watch TV. What does that mean?"

"I don't…"

"It *means,* you silly goose," (Emma didn't know why her version of Rachel called her that, it wasn't from the show, but she did), "that neither of them will be up until at least *twelve.*"

"So?"

"So you have *all the time in the world.* What does it take, ten minutes to walk to the mall from here? You could be there and back, like, twice, before they wake up!"

I mean I *could,* but…"

"But nothing! How many times have you had this dream?"

Emma thought about it. She didn't know, that was

the point. But…

"You've told me about it so many times even *I* know it off by heart; going to the shops on your own, buying whatever you want, never running out of cash, blah, blah, blah." Rachel wrinkled her nose at this last, so that Emma would know she wasn't being mean. "Well, here you go, girlfriend - start living the dream!"

Living the dream. Emma felt her heart pounding; the feeling, the *dream* feeling of walking through the shop, just taking anything that pleased her eye, with no need to even think about the price! The lightness, the joy, the freedom. It sang in her heart. Her eyes sparkled. And this time, when she thought *but I can't,* it felt thin, unconvincing.

Fully dressed, she returned to her bed and lifted the pillow. The bundles of notes lay side by side on her mattress. *Like cuddling kittens*, she thought. She reached out and touched them, feeling the reality of them against her fingertips. She smiled.

Sure, you can.

8:30 am

Henry blinked as he entered the train station, trying to adjust his vision to the fluorescent light. The fog that rendered the outside ghostlike and faintly unreal billowed through the automatic doors, melting away in contact with the warmer air.

London or Glasgow. That had been pinballing around his mind as he'd walked through the fog, cursing the rumbling of the wheels on the pavement. Glasgow felt safer; a city he'd never been in his life; zero danger of getting made. And cheaper, meaning getting a room somewhere without ID should be easier. On the other hand, the city still had a sizable heroin problem, and smackheads would happily rip off a shiny new case; especially if the guy wheeling it looked like he might be one of them; could rationalise it as stealing stolen goods, all that.

London, though. Cost an arm and a leg, but the risk of getting ripped off felt lower - place was CCTV city these days, especially around the stations, thank God for Al-Qaeda and all them fuckers. On the other hand, bit of a double-edged sword, potentially? Like, did Henry really need a transport policeman's attention? He did fucking not.

The dilemma rattled around, unresolved, and as Henry took in the handful of people milling around the ticket machines, and the single guy in a suit buying coffee at the kiosk, he made his decision; he'd catch the first available train, whichever direction. Pointless to wind himself up with this bullshit - the important thing wasn't *where,* the important thing was *away.*

He looked at the display board. The next train was due to leave from Platform 3 in eleven minutes. Final destination: Glasgow Central. Fair enough. Nice long journey. Spring for a couple of posh beers from the shop. Chill. Plan.

He wheeled the case over to the queue for the ticket desk; he didn't trust the machines with notes. The queue was only two deep, and he was soon standing in front of the window.

"How can I help you, sir?" The man was middle-aged, balding, half-moon glasses perched on the end of his nose. He hadn't yet looked up at Henry, which suited Henry just fine.

"Glasgow, please. Next available train."

"Return?"

"Single."

The man looked at Henry for the first time, peering over his glasses. His eyes flicked down to the notes in Henry's hand, then back up to his face. There was a hint of a smile as he asked "Standard, or First Class?"

First Class.

Henry had a sudden rush of memory: travelling with his mother to see his Nan up north, before things got bad; the train crowded, him and his younger brother out of sorts, bickering as soon as they got on board, a too-warm summer's day, and an announcement about 'weekend upgrade' and Mum saying, "Sod it" and taking them up to First Class.

The quiet tone. The cooler carriage with the bigger chairs. They'd grabbed an empty table seat, getting out their comics and games (Andy, Henry recalled, was still young enough for a colouring-in book, and he could suddenly picture his little brother, tongue sticking out as he tried to stay within the lines, a kaleidoscope of different coloured pens fanned out across the table's surface). Henry remembered a man in a suit with a funny looking newspaper (it had pink paper - *what kind of newspaper has pink paper?*) with a scrubbed pale face glaring at them, then rather grandly shaking the paper so it formed a barrier between them, *like a paper fort*, Henry thought, and laughed.

The memory of his laughter brought him back to the present. The ticket booth man was staring at Henry, his expression bored but not unkind, one eyebrow raised. Henry cleared his throat.

"Yes, right, sorry, yes please, First Class."

The ticket booth man shrugged, as if to say *none of my business, mate,* then clacked some buttons.

"That'll be two hundred and sixty pounds, sixty pence."

Henry felt a moment of dislocated shock. He closed his eyes and took a deep breath. *You can afford it. You've got money, now.*

He felt his heart hammering in his chest, but his hands were steady as he counted out the crisp twenty-pound notes. The ticket booth man slid the notes out onto his desk in a well-practised gesture and quickly thumbed through them, running what looked like a highlighter pen over the white space at the bottom centre of each. Henry's breath caught in his throat, and he felt his heart banging behind his ribs, heat flooding his cheeks, his mind just one word, stuck on repeat, *please, please, please…*

A few endless seconds later, the ticket booth man nodded, stacked the twenties, and slid them into a drawer. He counted out Henry's change while the machine spat out his tickets, placing both on the tray with a flourish and a perfunctory 'enjoy your journey'. Henry stammered out a 'thanks' he could barely hear over his own pulse and scooped the change into his fist, thrusting it into his trouser pocket. *It's all right, it's okay,* he thought, already turning, stalking towards the ticket barriers, eyes moving across the board, trying to make out which platform the Glasgow train was arriving at, cursing himself for not having checked before buying the ticket (forgetting he'd done exactly that, near-panic wreaking havoc on an already spotty short-term memory), willing his racing heart to slow the fuck down…

"Hey, sir!"

The voice was loud. Stern. Henry froze, even as his mind was screaming at him to run, just fucking run, take off! But where to? There'd be staff at the ticket barrier, and if he went back outside…

"Sir!"

Henry let out a shuddering breath, tears stinging his eyes, and turned around.

The ticket booth man was standing up, smiling. He jabbed his finger down, pointing through the Perspex screen.

"Isn't that your case, mate?"

8:35 am

Pete felt dirty. That was mainly because he *was* dirty; the hasty strip wash had gotten rid of the piss, but the skin of his chest, back, and legs still felt itchy, and his pubes felt like there was something crawling around in them; he had to suppress a groan as he realised that was possible, if not likely, given his activities of the previous evening.

He was also sweaty and out of breath from running up and down the stairs (of course the bastard lifts were out), his cheek and jaw were still sore from Mickey's slaps, and his hand ached from banging on Clive, Freddy, and Jim's front doors until they answered, each greeting him with a string of inventive swear words, complaints about the hour, and the opinion that "only fucking filth bang on a man's door like that, fer fuck's sake."

Apart from that, Pete thought, *everything's shit.*

None of them had known about the cases under their beds - or, in Jim's case, the sofa he'd slept on - which had also been an excruciating ball ache; having to have the same conversation three times with mostly asleep "mates", all hung over from their Saturday night excesses. The denial, accusations of being pranked, and then the inevitable barrage of questions Pete's own mind was equally crowded with, none of which he had any answers for. By the time he'd been through it for the third time with Jim, Pete was ready to slap someone in the face himself.

And now, here they all were; Clive, Freddy, Jim, Bobby B, Bobby D, Keef, and Billy. Everyone except Billy looked like shit warmed up, and Pete thought he'd never seen a room more in need of a gallon of ultra-strong coffee in his entire life.

They stood in a loose semicircle in Mental Mickey's living room. The glass coffee table that usually took up the centre of the room had been replaced with a neat stack of ten identical black suitcases. Looking at them made Pete feel ill, for a number of reasons; the sheer *impossibility* of them, a profound queasiness at being physically close to that much money (Pete felt somehow like the bags were glaring at him, or like he wasn't really looking at cases full of cash but unexploded bombs), and, above all, a dull stomach-churning rage. Because of *where* they were. Because of where *he* was.

Mental fucking Mickey's living room.

Pete remembered cancelling the cab to the airport, gut clenching as he stabbed the button on the app, a surge of stomach acid that almost made him gag.

There were leather sofas and chairs lining the walls,

but they all knew you didn't sit unless Mickey invited you to.

And he hadn't.

The man himself was standing in the doorway, looking them over, smiling, arms folded across his chest. Pete thought he looked like the Wish version of the governor from *Alien³*, but nothing about him, or the situation, was remotely funny.

"Well, lads. And Billy."

Mickey clapped his hands together. Every single bleary, bloodshot eye on him. Except Billy's, of course.

"We've got a busy morning ahead of us! There are one hundred and thirty-six flats in this building - eight per floor, seventeen floors. It's…" he flashed his hilariously chunky gold wristwatch "…eight thirty-seven. By ten, I want to have been inside every single one of those flats." He held his hands up as if to ward off an interruption, though as far as Pete could tell, nobody seemed to have any inclination to speak. "I know at least half the flats aren't occupied, so most likely there won't be cases in them, but I want to be sure. Could be squatters."

Mickey looked around. "I'm pairing you off. Clive, Freddy, you've got seventeen. Jim and Keef, sixteen. Billy and Pete, you take fifteen…"

"Fourteen."

Billy spoke without looking up from their phone.

The room had already been as hushed as a dozen men standing around in various states of semi-consciousness could be, but the quality of the silence changed, Pete thought. There were a couple of sharp intakes of breath. Pete found himself looking from Mickey to Billy, like he had seats to a particularly aggressive match at Wimbledon. Mickey's face was frozen, and Billy's didn't leave their phone screen.

Someone's going to die. Right here, in this room, right now, thought Pete. *Probably Billy.*

"Come again?" Mickey's voice was calm. Pete had half expected rage, or, worse, bonhomie. But Pete couldn't read Mickey's current tone at all, and that scared him badly. Mickey had a lot of, well, interesting qualities, but guile wasn't one of them. When you were as scary as Mickey, dissembling was something the other guy did.

Billy spoke, eyes still staring at the screen, "My flat's on fourteen, Mickey. Don't want Bobby anywhere near it. Either Bobby. No offence, lads." By the looks on their faces, Pete thought some was probably taken. At the same time, he could see Billy's point; the Bobbies were absolutely the most compulsive pair of thieves Pete had ever known. Their shared flat was stocked and decorated entirely with items they'd pilfered from neighbouring flats and businesses, including a wall-length oil painting of the previous landlord of The Orca, which they'd stolen from his apartment after he'd unwisely bragged about having it during one of his lock-ins. He'd disturbed them in the act, and they'd beaten him so badly he'd had to take early retirement. As Pete heard it, they hadn't even liked the man, yet every evening they ate their TV dinners under his slightly gormless smile, which, in Pete's opinion, just went to show that it takes all sorts of weird, twisted fucks.

And the two Bobbies definitely looked angry, Pete reflected, but also definitely looked shifty. Which, of course, they were, but…

Pete looked back at Mickey, who, to judge by his face, was reaching much the same conclusion as Pete had.

"You know what, Billy? That's a fair point. Now, lads and Billy, you all know each other's gafs, yes? So leave well alone, or you'll be answering to me. Understood?" Mickey was nominally addressing the group, but Pete noticed he'd not stopped staring at the two Bobbies the whole time, and that, aggrieved as they were acting, they couldn't meet his gaze for very long.

Mickey stared at the two Bobbies for a few more deeply uncomfortable seconds, then let out a deep sigh. "Yeah, okay, Billy and Pete, you take fourteen, Bobbys B and D, you're on fifteen. Everybody happy?"

Billy looked up from their phone, made eye contact with Mickey. "Thanks, boss."

"You're most welcome, Billy, now can I get fucking

on with it?"

The question was rhetorical.

Pete looked over at Billy, as Mickey started talking again. Their bright eyes shone out from under the brim of the dirty orange baseball cap they always wore. Billy looked back, nodded, a faint smile playing around their mouth. Then their gaze returned to the screen of their iMonstrosity. Pete nodded back, trying to keep his face neutral.

"Rich and Dave will stay on the ground floor, just in case any enterprising resident wakes up before we get to them and tries to leg it." *Or one of us tries the same, of course,* Pete thought, and a quick scan of the group confirmed that unhappy thought had indeed landed with a few of them. *You lot'd be well shit at poker.*

He glanced back at Billy, the only member of the crew who could get away with keeping their nose in their phone while Mickey was talking, let alone stand up to Mickey and retain the ability to chew solid foods. What, exactly, did the pairing signify? That Mickey didn't trust Pete? Or wanted Pete to keep an eye on Billy? Or fuck all?

Pete looked back at Mickey, whose gaze was moving restlessly from person to person as he continued his speech.

"The cases seem to appear underneath wherever someone is sleeping, so hit the bedrooms, and flip any sofas just in case. The good news is most people won't know it's there, so they won't know why *you're* there. Use masks. Clive'll pass them out as you leave. Bats and hammers, too. Crowbars - one per team. The doors and locks are for shit, so use the bars, then go in loud, scary, fast. Fear will do most of the work for you. Especially as you're not taking something they recognise as theirs. If someone tries to stop you, drop them hard enough to put off others. Leave the cases at the top of the stairs; runners'll bring them back here."

Mickey finally paused.

"The next bit's maths, so I'll say it slowly. Once you've done your floor, take four off the number you're on, go down to that floor, and continue."

Mickey snapped his fingers and pointed at Bobby D. "What floor are you on when you're finished?"

Pete actually saw the sweat pop out on Bobby's face, and he swallowed twice and licked his lips before answering, "Erm…eleven, Mickey."

"Good lad. And after that?"

"Erm, oh seven!"

Pete did the mental arithmetic and realised with a surge of relief that he and Billy would end up on six. His floor. No chance of anyone discovering Crazy Amy in his flat. Unless the racket of them going door to door woke her up, of course, but Pete was of the opinion that he'd burn that bridge when he got to it.

Mickey grinned. "See? Simples." His grin dropped, like someone had thrown a switch. "Ten AM, gents and Billy. I want every fucking case in the block. And someone will be checking the empty flats after. Any case that gets overlooked or left behind, the pair from that floor are going to be very sorry. Understood?"

Once more, Pete had cause to regret not getting into poker; he could have made a killing out of some of Mickey's crew. There were a lot of nods, not a lot of eye contact.

Except Billy. Billy was still staring at their phone.

"Any questions?"

"Erm…" It was Freddy, Pete saw, blushing furiously as he spoke, with an expression on his face that suggested he knew what he was doing was both stupid and dangerous, ".. so, do we actually know what the fuck is going on, though?"

Mickey looked at him.

"What's going on, Freddie, is that before the morning's over, we're all going to be multi-millionaires. Okay?"

"Yeah, no, sure, it's just…" Freddie looked to Pete like he might actually have a stroke before finishing his thought - *or maybe he's having one right now, and that's why he can't shut the fuck up* - but he continued "…like, where's the cash coming from? And, won't there be, I dunno…the government, and the rozzers and that, won't they…?" Freddy finally looked up from his scuffed sneakers and into Mickey's face, at which point his voice trailed off.

Mickey let the silence hang. There was a lot of foot shuffling. Most of the assembly suddenly found some aspect of the wall or ceiling drawing their concentrated attention. Pete watched the two men - Mickey, stonefaced, Freddy looking like he was hoping the ground would open up and swallow him - and wondered what Mickey would say. Because as much as Freddy was clearly regretting it, the question must have been in everyone's mind by this point.

Eventually. Mickey spoke. His voice was quiet.

"Freddy, who runs this block?"

"You do, Mickey."

"That's right, Freddy. You know why I run it?"

Freddy appeared to try to nod, shake his head, shrug, and bow, all at once. Under almost any other circumstances, Pete would have found it hilarious.

"It was rhetorical, you nonce." Still holding eye contact with Freddy, who looked to Pete like a man seconds away from a brain embolism induced by sheer terror, Mickey asked, "Billy? What's the internet saying?"

"Nothing, boss. BBC, ITV, Sky News, nothing. Even Twitter doesn't seem to have it." *And that's why Billy can get away with keeping their nose buried in their phone in the middle of a meet,* thought Pete, without rancour.

"Thank you, Billy." Mickey nodded, then held his hands out. "See?"

Freddy renewed his intense interest in his filthy trainers.

Mickey looked around the room as he spoke, making eye contact with anyone still looking at him. "I run this place, gentlemen and Billy, because when I'm faced with the opportunity of a lifetime, I don't waste a second asking stupid fucking questions about why. I grab it with both hands. And so will you." Mickey paused, placing his hands on his hips. "Get your shit together, and by the afternoon every single one of us is going to be rich enough to buy a tower each. That's it. Okay?"

Lots of nods, some mumbled, "Yes, Mickey"'s.

Mickey smiled. It was one of the scariest things Pete had ever seen.

"Good! Oh, Freddy did make one good point, though. While you're raiding the flats, if you see a phone, smash it. Slower word gets out, the better. Okay?"

More nods, the odd smile.

"Excellent. Don't forget, bats, bars, balaclavas in the kitchen. Grab 'em on the way out. Now fuck off and gather. Clock's ticking."

Pete looked at Billy. Billy looked back. Pete shrugged. Billy just smiled.

They joined the queue for the kitchen.

8:40 am

Emma walked through the fog, heart beating heavy in her chest, a mixture of exertion and fear. She'd seen from the car how thick it was - how it had covered the other side of the road, rendering the pavement and canal behind it invisible, swallowed by a wall of grey - but she hadn't realised how disorienting it would be to walk through. She knew she was heading in the right direction. There *was* only one path from her house to the city centre; a straight shot, albeit uphill and using a footpath that was constantly curving either towards or away from the main road, as it joined up with various underpasses that led to other estates.

But the fog was making her doubt herself.

She took a deep sniff from her sleeve, breathing in deep the perfume she'd sprayed there before leaving the house. It was orange blossom ('orange squash', Daddy Derek had called it once, before Mum shushed him), and branded with the Rachel logo from the TV show. It was Emma's favourite smell in the whole world, and normally it immediately calmed her down and cheered her up.

But not this morning.

It was the limited range of vision; *that* was the problem. She could see only as far as the faint glow of the next streetlight, still burning even though the sun was, theoretically, up there somewhere. She could hear traffic on the main road, but without being able to see it, she wasn't sure how far away it was; it sounded further away than it surely must be. She couldn't shift the idea that the path had gone *wrong;* that the fog was taking her *away,* somehow, leading her out into…what, exactly?

Stupid. That's stupid. You're fine. You know the way, you've done it before, you're not a baby, you're nine. It's just the fog.

She wished for what felt like the millionth time that she had a mobile phone to check the time on. She felt like she'd been walking for *ages,* but everything looked the *same,* it was like she'd just *left*…and underneath, there was the gnawing fear; all the dire warnings her mother had given her, about strangers, about going out alone…

She kept putting one foot in front of the other, hands thrust into the pockets of her too-thin coat, gripping the bundles of cash. That helped, a little; it was *real,* it was happening, she was *living the dream,* and that made her want to smile and feel a little sick, all at once. She wondered why Rachel, having talked her into this mad adventure, had been silent since she slipped out of the front door, leaving the door on the latch (but that was okay, nobody would be out in *this,* only crazy children who'd been visited early by the Christmas Suitcase Cash Fairy *[or Santa]* were out in *this*, and where, exactly...)

Her breath caught in her throat, her heart beating harder in her chest. Beyond the next streetlight, a familiar shape emerged from the fog. A few more steps, and she could see the side entrance to the shopping centre.

Emma let out a delighted giggle and spirited for the door. Then she was inside, walking down the wide, white corridor, her small steps echoing in the mostly empty space. The skin on her face tingled as the warm air blasted down from the overhead heaters. She took her hands out of her pockets, rubbing them together then shaking out her arms.

The clock on the electronic sign read 8:44. She stared down the mall, enjoying the sensation of being able to see at a distance again, and noted that none of the doors of the stores were open.

Well, okay. Most of them would open at nine. She could find a bench and sit until then.

She walked past the door of ToyZ N GamZ, eyes drawn to the window display; toys piled high in boxes at either side, figures from movies and cartoons, a track for toy cars she'd seen advertised so many times she knew the jingle by heart.

She caught herself doing the thing she always did;

looking at the toys but ignoring the price tags, knowing it was *all* too expensive, just trying to enjoy the sight of them…but, of course, today, *nothing* was too expensive, was it? If she liked the look of something, she could just…buy it. Right?

Sure, you can.

She made herself look at the prices. The Big Bad Toys from the CBBC alien invasion cartoons were £49.99 (she knew enough to know that meant £50, really). The racetrack was £200. She stared at it. It was massive, there was no way she could walk home with that under her arm, it'd take forever, she'd drop it. But…

Can I even afford it?

She glanced left and right, but the mall was still empty. She pulled a bundle out of her pocket and started counting.

Twenty, forty, sixty, eighty, one hundred, twenty, forty, sixty, eighty, two hundred.

She looked at the ten notes. She looked at the thickness of the remaining bundle.

She giggled. She couldn't help it.

Okay, but you've got to be able to get it all home. Hide it, somehow.

Yes, of course. She wasn't stupid. But…she thought maybe she could find a way to get that done.

Sure, you can.

Emma turned away from the window, heading to the nearby benches. She didn't see the figure inside the store that had watched her produce the bundle of cash and start counting it and was now tracking her as she skipped her way down the empty mall corridor.

8:45 am

Henry stared up at the electronic sign on Platform Four for what felt like the thousandth time, willing the seconds to tick by faster. He was sweating again, in spite of the persistent fog that shrouded everything, giving the station an otherworldly quality. He half remembered some short story he'd read as a kid about a train that took people to Hell. He imagined the weather looked quite a bit like this.

You're not going to Hell, mate. You're going to Glasgow. First class, no less. So, chin up.

Henry smiled to himself, but it was gone almost before it arrived. He tightened his grip on the suitcase handle, reminding himself it was there, he hadn't left it behind again. In truth, it hadn't left his grip since he'd retrieved it from in front of the ticket booth, the man behind it smiling politely as he not-quite-sprinted back to grab it. Recalling the moment sent another prickle of sweat into his armpits and across the brow of his hairline. He looked down at the giant coffee he'd bought at the platform kiosk (careful to pay using the change from the ticket purchase, keeping the rest of the notes out of sight), and was not surprised to see his hand trembling slightly, sending ripples across the surface of the steaming black fluid.

He raised it to his lips, blowing a couple of times before gingerly sipping. It still felt like imbibing lava, and it stung his tongue and throat as he swallowed, but the aftertaste was good, and he could feel the caffeine starting to work its magic, his thoughts turning over quicker.

He looked back at the clock.

8:46.

The train was still showing due at 8:48.

You've got this.

He started thinking about the next part; getting onboard (*first class, remember),* hoping it'd be empty enough he could keep the case with him, either in the seat next to him, or under his table if there was one free. He thought there would be; shouldn't be that many people travelling first class from Milton Keynes to fucking Glasgow three days before Christmas, surely?

Nah, he'd be fine: give the case the window seat, recline, relax, have a kip…no, maybe not that, the thought of waking up and the case not being there made Henry gulp nervously, and his grip flexed again on the handle, eyes flicking reflexively down to the large black shape at his heels.

Okay, no, no napping - maybe look at the free magazine, or a paper, even; the train started in London, maybe there'd be a *Metro* or *Evening Standard* to flick through.

Couldn't go to the buffet bar, of course, not with the case, but when the trolley service came by, Henry planned to absolutely rinse it; couple of rounds of posh sandwiches, crisps, choccy bars, few bevvies…

He thought about that more; pictured getting good and loaded as the train put hundreds of miles between him and MK and the underpass he'd been living under, arriving at Glasgow drunk enough to either leave the case on the train or be the easiest mark imaginable as he disembarked…

8:47

…okay, take two: yes to the window seat for the case, yes to rinsing the trolley, but just the grub and a few cans of Coke, ride out the sugar and caffeine buzz all the way to bonnie Scotland, then march up to the black cab rank, ask to be taken to a hotel that didn't need photo ID to check in; tip the cabbie a wink and an extra tenner, check in, stick the cash in the room safe, Shower for an hour, sleep for a week, and then…

"Excuse me, sir?"

The words fell on Henry like a hammer. The voice was male, polite, faintly bored, and very, very official. Henry turned his head towards the source of the statement, hoping for either a barista or ticket inspector.

His eyes took in the black uniform, the words Thames Valley Police picked out in white across the man's chest.

Fuck.

His eyes moved up further. The man was taller than Henry, perhaps six feet. He was clean-shaven, but Henry took in a very faint line of stubble, which, alongside the bags under the eyes, suggested that the officer had been on duty overnight. The eyes themselves were brown and alert, and Henry saw a lock of dark hair that had slipped from under the officer's hat.

Henry felt like he was shrinking.

"Yes, officer? How can I help?" Henry hated the tremble he heard in his voice, but couldn't do anything to stop it. *Not fair! So close!*

"Do you mind telling me where you're travelling to today?"

Fuck off fuck off fuck off….

"Glasgow, as it happens. My train's about to arrive." *Any second now'd be ideal.*

"I see, sir." There was a pause, and Henry could hear the roar of the train approaching.

"And is that your case?"

"Yes! It is!" Too loud, too angry. The officer took a half step back, one hand moving to his belt. Henry took a deep breath, willed himself not to move, every nerve ending screaming at him to run, push the copper over and leg it…*So*

close!

"Could you tell me what's in it, then, please?"

Henry sagged, feeling suddenly lightheaded, the exertion of the walk to the station, the stress of nearly leaving the case behind, and the strong coffee on an empty stomach combining in a wave of nausea. He looked at the case, then slowly back at the officer.

The roar of the train grew louder.

Henry stared. He couldn't think of anything to say.

"Step away from the platform, please, sir." The policeman had to raise his voice to be heard over the train engine.

Henry hung his head, then nodded. He turned away as the train slammed past him, the wind of its passing ruffling his hair and flapping his coat.

As he walked towards the officer, away from the Glasgow train, a single tear ran down his cheek.

Luke watched the man approach, keeping his face impassive. *Sure, he's sad now he's been caught,* he thought, but there was something pathetic about the man; his clothes were dirty and obviously slept in, and his face was clearly showing pain - maybe regret, but maybe not just that. *Okay, but if you're hungry, there's places you can get fed. No call to be nicking people's suitcases.*

Luke raised a hand, and the man stopped a few feet away. Close enough for Luke to get a decent whiff of body odour. Definitely slept in the clothes, and not his first night, either. Still...

"Do you mind telling me where you got the case, sir?"

The man's shoulders slumped further, and Luke saw something he'd seen many times, usually just before he slipped the cuffs on someone. His hand reached instinctively for his belt.

"Found it."

Luke nodded. He'd heard that one a few times, too.

"Where did you find it?" He felt like slipping in a mate at the end of the sentence, but decided not to risk it. Sometimes it would come over friendly, but sometimes it could feel confrontational. Besides, in Luke's estimation, the man had given up - and under those circumstances, offering a friendly platitude might accidentally put some steel back in the man's spine.

"Under my tent. Where I was sleeping."

That is *a new one,* Luke reflected, though admittedly a variation on an ever-popular theme.

"What's your name?"

"Henry."

"Okay, Henry, I've stopped you on suspicion of handling stolen goods, okay? I'm going to take a look in the case, now. Want to tell me what I'm going to find? Anything that could cause me harm?"

Henry shook his head and burst into tears.

8:50 am

Pete looked up at Billy and adjusted his grip on the crowbar, driving the business end deeper into the wood around the door lock. He stared at Billy's hand as they counted down from three with their fingers, feeling the adrenaline surging into his system, tweaking like he'd done a line of Mickey's good speed.

It was their sixth door. Pete couldn't believe how easy it was going. Sure, three of the five flats they'd entered were empty, which helped; the last had shown signs of squatters (sheets nailed over the living room windows and a mattress with stains on it Pete didn't want to think about, or for that matter smell, ever again), but no cases. They'd moved quickly room to room to make fucking sure, Mickey's warning booming in Pete's memory. He was already halfway down shit street just by the fact of having two cases, and if Mental Mickey should uncover the identity of the 'slapper' Pete had picked up last night...

Three empty. One occupied by some long-haired stoner with a ratty goatee who, Pete guessed, might still not have fully woken up. He'd certainly slept through Billy taking the door (by silent agreement, Pete and Billy alternated opening duty, the other using the bat as threat/deterrent), and seemed no more than semi-awake even after Pete had flipped the cheap chipboard bedframe (tumbling the man and his rumpled bedding out onto the floor in the process), and grabbed the black case underneath. By the time the man had mumbled something that at least resembled "What the fuck?" and clawed his way back to the surface of his upended sleeping arrangements, Pete, Billy and the case were already out of the flat.

The door before this one had been tougher; a mother and two kids, one primary school age, one barely a toddler. She'd been awake, in the kitchen, and her 'what the fuck?' had been rather louder and more heartfelt than stoner boy. Pete had slapped the cheap-looking smart phone out of her hand and stomped it into the linoleum, prompting a shriek of fury from the woman. The kids had looked up from their seats on the sofa, frozen in the act of shovelling cornflakes into their mouths, and the synchronised bursting into tears might, under other circumstances, have seemed comic. Billy pushed through to the two bedrooms while Pete attempted to calm the woman, first by placation, then by threatening to hit her with the fucking bat if she didn't fucking sit down. That prompted another howl from the children, and for a second, Pete thought about threatening them with a beating, but a memory rose up of his father's angry face threatening to beat the shit out of him until he was screaming if he ever did that again, and he shut his mouth, sick to the stomach with shame and fear.

What the fuck am I doing?

Billy came back with one case and shrugged at Pete's glance. Pete thought about going back and double-checking, Mickey's threats bubbling up again, but the idea of checking Billy's homework felt…uncomfortable. *Fucked either way,* he thought, the sick feeling in his stomach curdling. Fucked all ways. Just…fucked.

As they took the cases over to the stairs for the runners (who in Pete's opinion, were displaying far too much spunk for a Saturday fucking morning in Melrose Tower), and also when they were walking between doors, Billy's phone was out, thumbs moving at an alarming rate, sites flicking past so quickly Pete had no idea how Billy was taking anything in. On the way to door number six, Pete asked what the internet was saying, and Billy's "Nothing" was final enough that Pete didn't follow up.

Now, seeing Billy signal three, Pete pulled hard on the crowbar, the splintering sound of the wood around the lock sending another surge of adrenaline into his body, lending strength to his shoulder as he slammed it against the door, forcing it open.

Momentum carried him five steps into what should have been the kitchen area of the flat. With each step, his sense of disorientation grew.

The space was huge. Not just bigger than the kitchen should be, but wider than the entire flat. To his left the space ended with the connecting wall, and the flat that contained the angry women and howling kids (Pete realised, distractedly, that he could still hear their muffled crying through the wall, over the sound of the kids channel cartoons), and to his right, the room - the single room - just seemed to go on and on.

The space had to be at least two flats knocked through. Maybe three or four.

It was hard to tell, even with the glaring overhead lighting, because most of the floor was taken up with large black plastic tubs that looked to Pete like wheelie bins that had been sawn off part way up, out of which were growing the largest marijuana plants Pete had ever seen.

"What the fuck?" Pete whispered, barely registering the door closing behind him, mind spinning, gears slipping; desperately trying to assimilate what his senses were telling him.

An indoor cannabis farm, taking up about a quarter of floor fourteen of Melrose Tower.

A cannabis farm that Mickey didn't know about?

Couldn't know about. No way he'd have sent Billy and

Pete to raid it, *so who the fuck...?* Pete started to think.

Too late, his mind registered that the door had been closed behind him, and Billy was striding towards him.

Billy. Billy's flat. Why Billy wanted floor fourteen. Fuck. *Fu...*

Pete started to turn his head, his mouth dropping open to say something he'd not yet formulated. The crowbar caught him square on the temple. Pete was aware only of a loud, solid crunch, like a car boot being slammed shut, and a flash of light.

He was dead before he hit the ground.

Billy exhaled for a slow count of five while they looked down at the body. Body? Billy thought so. The impact of the crowbar on Pete's skull had felt fairly final; the jolt had run right up to Billy's shoulder. Still, they took the five count, watching the blood pooling under Pete's head. *No time to mop this up; the rozzers will suss he was killed in here,* Billy reflected, which was, of course, true, but also probably didn't matter in the grand scheme of things. For one, they were going to be very, very busy today, Billy guessed. For another, Billy intended to be a very, very long way away from Melrose Tower before they turned up with their blue lights and questions.

No, Billy's only concern was how they could cover this with Mental Mickey long enough to get the fuck out of town.

Billy had been worrying at the problem ever since they'd been attached to Pete. Arguing successfully for floor fourteen had been the key. The cases were a once-in-a-lifetime chance to leave all of this behind, Billy saw that immediately; but the discovery of their floor fourteen farm would have comprehensively fucked it.

Billy ran it through their mind one more time, then shrugged. They hadn't set the table, but the cards were well and truly in the air. *You can always get beat. Nature of the game. Don't beat yourself. Make them beat you.*

Billy searched Pete's pockets, finding his flat key in the right-hand pocket of Pete's ragged puffer jacket. Billy took it and, after a second's internal debate, pocketed it.

Billy drew a knife from their boot. It was a dirty-looking street blade, highly illegal, and nobody on Melrose had ever seen Billy so much as flash it.

Billy used the blade to rip the sleeve of their jacket above the elbow, scratching the skin underneath without drawing blood. Then they got their arms under Pete's armpits and dragged him towards the door.

He went for me with the knife. We wrestled.

Billy opened the door to the flat, checking left and right. Nobody. The case couriers were waiting in the middle landings of each stairwell so they could cover collections from two floors at once, and, in any case, the fog was obscuring the top of the steps.

Good deal.

Billy went back to Pete. The body was heavy, and Billy noticed with a snarl of distaste that Pete's bowels had released, giving off a rank foulness that almost made Billy wish they could kill him again.

He went for me with the knife. We wrestled. He went over the balcony.

Would it fly? Billy thought it would.

If Billy could answer the next, obvious question: *Why?*

Billy had an answer to that, too. It was risky, but so was the whole mess. And their window was very, very narrow, now. Besides, Billy loved her. And this was how they could get them both out clean.

Because he knew I knew he'd slept with Crazy Amy.

Billy thought that'd fly just fine, at least for as long as they needed it to.

Which was more than they could say for Pete.

Billy hoisted Pete over the balcony, placing the knife loosely in Pete's hand. It'd fall out before he hit the ground, most likely, but that didn't matter.

By the time the sound of Pete's body landing on a parked vehicle with an almighty crash made it back up to the fourteenth floor, Billy was already jogging towards the stairwell, calling calmly for help.

8:55 am

Emma sat on the cold metal bench, feet swinging, watching the door of ToyZ N GamZ, willing the gate to slide all the way up, the lights at the front of the shop to come on. She'd seen people arriving for work, coats over the black shirts with the cartoon giraffe logo that Emma thought was so cool, and she'd engaged in a happy daydream where, like Rachel, she worked here instead of going to boring old school, getting to wear a special shirt and be amongst the toys all day, demonstrating how they worked to the other kids and telling the parents how brilliant the toys were. *Basically just like being able to play all day, how cool?* She thought, knowing even at nine years old it probably wasn't *really* like that, but enjoying the fantasy.

As the daydream played out, her hand stole into her pocket and riffled the bundle of paper - a movement that had already become a compulsion - as she assured herself this was *real,* that she really was about to start *living the dream.*

And then Rachel was sitting next to her, grinning that toothy grin. Emma grinned back and started talking to her; describing all the toys she could think of, what she might buy (she had to plan; nothing she couldn't carry). "Sure, but they have *bags,* you can carry a lot, you're strong as an *ox!*" Rachel said, which cracked Emma up.

Emma sat and talked with Rachel, watching the employees arrive (her eyes, focussed on their shirt logos, not taking in their tired, lined faces, puffy eyes, nor the careful, economical movements of people who know they are going to be on their feet for much of the next twelve hours. None of the opening shift ToyZ N GamZ staff had been asleep at 8:04am this midwinter morning, every single one had already been awake, getting ready for work and worrying about the commute; no suitcases under these beds), and she'd noticed the security gate that raised and lowered, allowing them into the store.

She couldn't see the man operating it, because he was in the unlit shadows on the other side of the gate, and the angle was wrong.

But he could see her. Very clearly.

Keith Winters, Security Guard, 47, had been in the building since 6 a.m - an hour earlier than his contract required. The company didn't pay him for the extra hour, but it was the time he'd told his wife he started, and the other employees never knew, because they also weren't there when he *was* supposed to start, at seven, so what did it matter? He had a cover story, if anyone higher up the food chain ever noticed, But Keith doubted he'd ever need it.

That suited Keith just fine.

It suited Keith for two reasons; one, it gave him a guaranteed uninterruptible hour during which he could indulge an internet porn habit that had become so routine that he would often yawn as he jerked it to increasingly topic-focussed videos of young women being sexually exploited (either by their landlords, in lieu of overdue rent or, in his favourite sub-genre, for obvious reasons, by security guards who had caught them shoplifting, with the threat of the cops compelling fellatio, usually followed by a rough raw dog bent over a desk). The ones that looked like they were crying were his favourites. Sometimes he'd even yawn when he came, though he wasn't aware of the fact. And two, it was an hour less he had to spend with his fucking wife Jenine, and his idiot kid Patsy.

Patsy had been an accident. Keith had been slipping it to Jenine for years, on the quiet while her old man was around, then with increasing frequency and vigour after he'd died of cancer. The arrangement had suited Keith well; she'd lived a few doors down, so sneaking about on her husband had been relatively easy (and, Keith had to admit to himself, part of the turn on - God knew she wasn't much to look at from the neck up). He'd intended to break it off once he'd died, but she'd been more welcoming than ever, her edge of desperation and widow status proving even more of a turn on. Keith enjoying finding increasingly degrading and aggressive ways to fuck her in her dead husband's house…

And then Patsy happened. A fucking miracle, apparently, given the years Jenine had been trying with her dead husband (and Keith's occasional enthusiastic assistance; what a joke that would have been, he'd often thought, if old Bill had had to bring up Keith's brat as his own - he'd sometimes think about that as he came inside Jenine, back in the day, and it always made him smile). But the joke had been on Keith, apparently. His dad, long dead from cancer, had always been very clear on the matter of children - *"you knock some girl up, Keith, you'd better fuckin' marry her,"* and Keith agreed with that completely. Too many single mums out there, their own faults, of course, dumb sluts, getting knocked up for a free flat, but Keith knew his obligations, so when Jenine had given him the news, he'd popped the question. She'd practically bitten his hand off.

The sex that evening had been pretty good (though she'd taken the lead a bit too much for Keith's taste - he'd enjoyed her like that when she'd been cheating on Bill, but it wasn't, he thought, how a *faithful* married woman should behave), but it had also marked the beginning of the end.

The pregnancy, after an initial couple of weeks of glow, took a turn for the worse; Jenine got increasingly irritable and argumentative. Keith remembered the good old days, when he'd head over steaming drunk on a Sunday afternoon, burst in the door (after Bill had died, of course, or when he'd been away on business), tell her to drop her knickers and just bend her over the sofa till he was done. She'd always done as she was told (it was her only really attractive trait, in Keith's opinion) but with a baby inside her, it was different. Couldn't risk hurting the kid.

It got worse as the pregnancy progressed - terrible sickness, tits swollen (Keith only had to look at 'em for her to start getting all weepy), and then the fucking hernia, and the piles, couldn't even put it up her arse anymore, months of trying to work out excuses to go into the garden shed so he could have a quick wank to PornHub.

And then Patsy had been born, and Keith thought things would get back to normal, but there had been "significant tearing," according to the hospital, meaning Jenine's vag was *still* a no-cock zone. One night, Jenine back from hospital maybe two weeks, Keith had had enough; back after a late one at the pub (fucking Tottenham had fucked it again, bunch of fairies and coons they had playing for them that season, pathetic), he'd stormed into the bedroom and not even waited for her to wake up properly, just put her on her back and stuck it in, ignoring her cries and screams until the baby joined in, and then Keith suddenly found he couldn't any more, too much fucking racket.

He'd slept on the sofa that night. Jenine had to go back to the doctors, then the hospital, and it was made very clear to Keith and Jenine that further "sexual activity" would have to wait until she was properly healed. The doctor (some black bitch with dreads and round glasses, like she thought she was John fucking Lennon or some shit) was talking to both of them, but she kept staring at Keith, and Keith smiled a tight smile and nodded back, fist closing around his car keys in his pocket, fantasising about punching the bitch in the face with them, making holes in her cheeks and chin and forehead, slapping her glasses off and putting his car key right through one of her fucking eyes…

They drove home in silence. Jenine tried to apologise, twice, but Keith shut her off.

From then on, not only could he not get hard, he felt his dick and balls shrink every time he looked at his wife. He'd thought about forcing himself on her again, once months had gone by and she'd healed, but he just…couldn't. The face of that black bitch would rise up in his mind, and though he was able to indulge a series of incredibly violent sexual encounters with *her* (about which, afterwards, he'd feel shame for indulging even in the fantasy of something he found as abhorrent and perverse as race mixing), for his wife there was nothing but this shrivelled anti-boner that made him want to slit his own fucking throat.

And then he'd lost his white van delivery driver job; finally got caught red-handed offloading two pallets of fresh food at the market that he was supposed to be delivering to one of the posh downtown delicatessens, (and fuck whoever dobbed him in on that one). He noticed his status at The Orca had taken a bit of a nosedive after that, now he was no longer the source of regular trays of scotch eggs or ten tubs of potted shrimp for a pint (fucking bunch of fair-weather so-called "mates," wouldn't piss on them if they were on fire). He'd even had to bribe Dodgy Del (owner of the imaginatively titled Del's Motors, definitely the most bent second-hand car/garage combo unit in Bletchley, if not the entire county) into providing him with a fake reference to get a job stopping teenagers robbing fucking Pokémon cards.

But it was a living; kept him in beers and fags. He started taking his "early shifts" not long after. Jenine didn't seem to mind.

Seven years of his life had gone by. His missus wasn't getting it from him, nor anywhere else, as far as he could tell (and given his prior experience, Keith felt sure he *would* know). She didn't seem to miss it. Didn't seem to miss him. *A loveless marriage*, thought Keith, meaning of course a fuckless marriage, love being a concept essentially alien to him.

Still, it wasn't so bad. Beers with Dodgy Del, Mental Mickey (when the fucker felt like turning up, and wasn't on a ban for calling the landlady a cunt) and the rest of the boys at the weekend. The early start and good long wanks in the staff room (getting a smart TV in there had been a touch, being able to broadcast that filth from his phone onto the bigger screen was genius, who said the eggheads never did nothing good?). Having a daughter was the final kick in the nuts, of course (the way things were, no chance of a boy to balance the scales), but Jenine did all the kid and girly stuff. As long as Keith was earning she didn't seem to mind.

That's what Keith thought he felt, on the morning of December 22nd, year of Our Lord, 2019.

Until he saw a little girl at the shop window, maybe only a year or two older than his own kid, counting out twenties in a bundle bigger than her fist, and showing a bulge in her coat pocket that suggested there was more - a lot more - where that came from.

As the minute hand on the big clock over the door rolled over, marking the arrival of 9:00 am and the store opening, he turned the key to open the security gate, the girl already half skipping, half running through the door, weaving past the other bedraggled last-minute bargain hunters. At that moment, Keith felt nothing more complicated than rage. At the child's happiness. At her apparent good fortune.

She's far too young to be carrying that kind of cash.

The thought sat, and expanded, until, quite suddenly, the scale of it - and of what it might mean - obliterated everything else from Keith's mind.

Where did you get that money, little one? He thought, completely unaware of the grin that had broken out across his face, as bright and brittle as broken glass, only dimly aware that his penis was stirring into a sluggish semi-erection.

Hour 2

9:00 am - 10:00 am

9:00 am

As he pulled away from the railway station, Luke stole another glance in the rearview mirror at Henry, shoulders hunched, slanted forward to try to accommodate his cuffed hands. He'd been careful when radioing into control not to give too much information, only mentioning "a quantity of cash that the suspect couldn't account for" - not because he had any intention of skimming (the thought had genuinely not crossed Luke's mind; one look at the quality and neatness of the bills made it clear that there was a precise amount involved, here, and, wherever Henry had actually acquired it, knowing what that precise figure was might end up being a crucial piece of evidence), but because whatever *was* going on here, it was clearly far, far bigger than Henry the homeless man, and his "lucky find".

Besides, thought Luke, as he turned out onto the wide, double-lane road that would take him most of the short ride back to the station, *I'm not a fucking thief.*

But was Henry?

Luke's gut said yes; but it wasn't a concrete certainty, and there were many unanswered questions if Henry *had* taken it.

Such as…

"Who does the case belong to, Henry?"

It was a tricksy question, almost forcing Henry into a lie which Luke thought he had a reasonable chance of spotting, and which could be usefully leveraged later. Henry didn't exactly seem like a criminal mastermind.

"I have no idea! I told you…"

"You just found it under your tent?"

"Yes!"

"You were sleeping in the tent?"

"Yes."

Luke frowned. It was such obvious bullshit, which bothered him. Henry was clearly not Mensa material, but he wasn't an outright imbecile, either, nor obviously brain damaged from substance abuse. Yet it felt like a junkie lie, to Luke: stubborn but nonsensical. Because, well…

"How did somebody get it under your tent without waking you up?"

Henry laughed. It was a dry, painful sound. "It's worse than that; how did it end up not just under my tent but under *me?*' Henry held Luke's eye until Luke had to redirect his attention to the road, and Luke was disconcerted to realise that he couldn't read Henry at all. None of the obvious "I'm lying" tells were flashing. But the story still felt…*wrong*.

Luke changed tack. "Are you lying to me, Henry?"

Henry met his eyes, then looked out the window. "No." His voice was soft, sad. Luke didn't like the shifty eye contact, but he'd seen that often enough from people simply nervous of the uniform not to read too much into it.

"Do you trust me, Henry?"

"Of course, you're a police officer."

Luke looked up sharply at that last, antennae twitching like crazy, but Henry had rested his head against the window and was staring out at the rolling fog with an expression on his face that looked sad, disengaged. Which reminded Luke of something he should have asked earlier; would have asked, if the contents of the suitcase hadn't temporarily caused part of his brain to short circuit.

"Are you on anything you shouldn't be on, Henry? Smoked any weed, done a line, anything?"

"No."

"We'll test you when we get back to the station, so if there *is* anything…"

"There isn't. I haven't even had a drink."

Luke shrugged. That seemed unlikely, but it wasn't unheard of. Anyway. Swing and a miss on trust bonding over substance abuse. He drove in silence for a few seconds, trying to work out what to ask next. *Should have a partner doing this, let me concentrate on the driving,* he thought, angry all over again at

Steve's plausibly deniable "stinking head cold" that just happened to have hit him in time to miss his final overnight before Christmas. Not enough he'd gotten the day itself as leave *again,* despite Luke making sure he'd put his application in early this year, hoping for some quality time with Rob, who always got so down this time of year, but to pull a sickie just before…*He'll probably be back on the 27th and moan about how ill he's been all Christmas,* thought Luke, hands tightening on the wheel as he imagined his partner's face creased in a frown, those little bastard eyes twinkling…

"All units, all units, armed robbery in progress, Santander Bank, city centre, officer down, officer down, code red…"

The rest of the call was drowned out by the sound of the sirens and the roar of the engine as Luke floored the accelerator, pulling a screaming U-turn tight enough to send Henry flying across the back seat, banging into the far side door.

"Hang on back there," Luke said, mind racing ahead, adrenaline surging through his system.

9:05 am

Billy eased the key into the lock on Pete's flat, then gently turned it.

A stupid risk, Billy knew that - and given Mickey's current mood, dangerous - but a pretty small one. With Pete's body going over the balcony and everyone being in such a damn hurry, odds were nobody would notice Billy hadn't kicked the door in. Even if they did, Billy could say that they'd banged on the door and Amy had let them in.

Must remember to tell her that, Billy thought, turning the latch to shut the front door quietly before making their way across the kitchen. The living room door was ajar. Billy pushed it open, taking in the scene.

The layout of the room was familiar from last night's live viewing, but the angle was different enough to create a moment of disorientation. Billy scanned the far wall, eventually spotting it; a barely discernible bulge under the Prodigy poster above the television. Billy couldn't see it from this distance, but they knew there was a small hole in the poster. It was through this hole that the webcam Amy had installed a few days ago had recorded and broadcast her stoned seduction of Pete the previous night to Billy's laptop a few floors up.

Billy gave themself one slow breath to enjoy the memory, allowing the smell of stale weed, sweat, and piss to add detail to what they'd only been able to see last night (Billy had asked Amy why there was never any sound on the footage, but all she'd ever said on the subject was "I like thinking about you imagining what noises I'm making," which Billy found simultaneously intensely frustrating and horny as hell). Billy thought about the way Amy had led Pete around, literally and metaphorically by the dick, blissfully unaware that he was being posed for Billy's benefit. Taking the scene in, Billy realised Pete had likely been staring at his own reflection in the TV screen, not realising Amy's smile and wink before she put him in her mouth, or the open-mounted grin as she'd bent herself over the sofa were there for Billy's enjoyment. And, of course, for Amy and Billy to enjoy together later.

Probably not this particular recording, though thought Billy, with a twinge of regret. It had been a vintage Amy performance; inventive, playful, and absolutely filthy, and Pete's highly intoxicated state ("I always tell them it's Rohypnol, it's not my fault they think it's actually wizz or E," Amy had said, giggling, when Billy first questioned her about why the men she made the films with were always so out of it) added a level of comedy gold to the proceedings.

Then Billy thought about their last look at Pete as he plummeted over the balcony. The mist swallowing him up. The crunch of the body hitting what Billy now knew was Clive's beloved Audi.

Yeah, probably not this particular recording.

Billy reached out gently, their fingertips stroking Amy's shoulder, even with the enormous time crunch unwilling to rush the moment. Amy slept deep, and watching her wake was one of Billy's favourite things.

Billy placed their hand on Amy's shoulder, gripping softly. They gave a gentle shake, saying her name. She scrunched up her eyes, curling into a ball on her side, the motion pulling down the sheet, revealing the pale skin of her back, and Billy's breath caught, as it often did. Billy loved Amy for every aspect of her, inside and out. They loved that Amy was the only person that had never shown the slightest interest in what was in Billy's pants, they loved Amy's unapologetic and untamed sexual appetites…and, Billy had to concede to themself, the physical package that contained all those things they loved was also exquisite.

But the clock was ticking.

"Amy." Billy said it louder, placing their hand on Amy's cheek, stroking her cheekbone with their thumb, feeling a surge of love and lust even through the fear.

"Billy," Amy replied, a sleepy smile stretching across

her face, eyes still shut. "Why are you waking me up?"

Billy waited. Amy's frown deepened, then her brows rose, and her eyes opened, widened with shock - so brown they were almost black, dark pools Billy felt they could swim in forever - and her smile dropped away. "Billy, what the fuck?"

Billy waited. They saw Amy's pupils dilate as she focussed on Billy, then her jaw dropped slightly, her voice softening, hand already moving to Billy's bruised face.

"Billy, what the fuck?"

"Mickey."

"The fuck?" There was anger in her voice. No fear. Billy loved her so much for that. "Why? He doesn't know…about…" she gestured at the flat, the wall, the camera, with one sweep of her arm. She was sat up now, and the movement caused the sheet to fall away from her chest. Billy focused all their considerable will in maintaining eye contact, ignoring the siren call of their peripheral vision.

"Listen, lover. I really need you to focus, okay? I think I've found our way out, but we're going to have to take some chances, and we don't have much time."

As if to emphasise the statement, a staccato flurry of blows rattled the front door in its frame.

"I'm here! I've got her, tell Mickey I've got her, she's gone to the bathroom. Two minutes!"

"No time for that shit, Billy. We've got to move." Bobby D's voice was loud enough that the tremble in his voice, fear as well as anger, rang out to Billy as clear as a bell.

"You want to drag her off the crapper with her knickers around her ankles, be my guest!"

That drew a pause. Mickey's orders had been clear - get Amy out of Melrose as soon as possible - but equally clear was what happened to anyone who caused Amy any kind of discomfort. It was pretty unfair, reflected Billy, but then Mickey was a master at making things other people's problems.

Amy grabbed Billy's shirt collar and pulled them close. "You can drag me off the crapper with my knickers around my ankles anytime." Her words were delivered with a breathy whisper and a tight grin that tickled Billy's ear and set their stomach and groin tightening.

"All right, tell her to fucking hurry up!" Bobby D, implementing his own version of Mickey's "shit runs downhill" approach to delegation.

"Two minutes!" Billy yelled back. Then, softly "Amy, you have to get dressed, okay? We've got to get out of here and I can't concentrate while you're…"

Amy kissed Billy's cheek, then said "We're really getting out?"

"I think so."

"Tell me." She'd already slid from under the sheets, and as Billy started to talk, she located her knickers and bra (hanging from a very sorry-looking wooden lamp next to the TV) and put them on. Billy tried to ignore the mesmerising, high-speed reverse striptease and marshal their thoughts. They'd had a few precious seconds to think about it on the way down from Mickey's flat after explaining what had happened to Pete, trying to ignore the painful swelling on their face, trying to shake the memory of Mickey's fists colliding with their cheek and chin, Billy concentrating all their will into two imperatives - keeping on their feet, and not swinging back, no matter how confident they were that they could knock Mickey into the middle of next week in a fair fight. And they'd decided to start at the end and work backwards, because, they reluctantly concluded, it made the most sense.

So, tell her, Billy. Time's ticking.

"Mickey's getting the two Bobbys to move us out of the flats."

"Why?" She shrugged into her ancient Nine Inch Nails T-Shirt, a trophy from one of her earlier encounters, as Billy answered.

"Because he thinks the feds are going to be here any minute."

"A raid?"

"Murder investigation."

Amy paused for just a second, then continued pulling up her jeans. "Who?"

"Pete."

Amy's jaw clenched and she stared straight ahead, eyes practically burning a hole in the wall, hands balled into fists. Not looking at Billy, she growled through gritted teeth "Because of me? Mickey..."

"No. It was me. I broke his skull with a crowbar, then dropped him over the balcony."

Amy turned to Billy. Her jaw unclenched, fists straightening back into hands. "Explain."

Billy took a deep breath. *Here we go.*

"I had to."

"I know that. Explain."

I love you so much, Billy thought.

"I couldn't keep him away from the farm. We were up there on Mickey's orders."

Amy knew about the farm, of course. Amy knew who Billy's *real* crew was; knew Billy's job was to monitor the Melrose psycho, make sure he didn't get any ideas above his station or outside his building. Fine if the local druggies were prepared to brave the piss-soaked stairwells for an overpriced baggie, as long as Mickey didn't move his particular brand of dealing and lending with menaces past The Orca and into the city centre pubs and clubs where the *real* action was.

Billy had shared it all with her, as they'd lain wrapped around each other under the giant duvet, passing a joint made from freshly harvested product back and forth; Billy's job a punishment for their refusal to let go of their identity, but also a backhanded compliment, an acknowledgement of the skills Billy brought to the table. The farm part "fuck you" to Mickey, rival firm growing superior gear right under his nose, part "fuck you" to Billy (manage this well or die, freak), but also an insurance policy. Mickey didn't know it, but, on paper, the fourteenth floor flats Billy lived in were actually owned by Mr. Mental. An efficient way to pull the plug on him quickly, should the need arise. Billy's ever-present laptop bag and known habit of wandering the streets at all hours gave them the ability to move the product out, at small scale, with impunity.

Amy knew that Billy wanted out from all of it; Mickey, their old crew, the farm, Melrose, Milton fucking Keynes. And they wanted to take her with them.

"Mickey knows about the farm?" Amy's fist was knuckling her eye, and the word "farm" turned into a confused yawn. Billy just stared. "No, okay, because he'd have dropped *you* over a balcony, not given you a couple of love taps before sending you to pick me up. So…"

"Amy, this is the mental bit, okay? I swear every word is true…"

"Don't waste my time, Billy. Explain."

Billy grinned.

"At some point overnight - nobody knows exactly when or how - suitcases have been appearing under beds, mattresses, sofas...wherever people have been sleeping. Suitcases full of cash."

Billy paused, feeling the weight of the weirdness hit them full force for the first time. They'd been so preoccupied with the sheer kinetic energy of the morning, and trying to stay one step ahead of Mickey's insane scheme, that they'd not really had time to take in the cosmic insanity of...

"The money's real?"

Billy snapped back to the here and now, catching Amy's eye. "Looks that way. I ran a couple of serial numbers from bills in the cases, they came back real. But, Amy, there's a million quid in each suitcase. So, I mean..."

"Yeah, even if it's got legit numbers, the feds will have to make it not real, somehow. Oh, motherfucker!" Amy flipped the mattress she'd just vacated, then looked at Billy. "Pete?"

"Pete. He turned up at Mickey's with two cases."

She nodded, a smile playing at the corner of her mouth. "Wish I could have heard how he explained that to brother dearest. Must have been shitting himself. You could almost feel sorry for the twat. Okay, so...Mickey wanted all the cases, got you lot all together to go door to door and take them all?"

"Yup. I talked Mickey into giving Pete and I floor fourteen, but…"

"But you couldn't stop Pete taking the door two away from your flat."

"Nope."

"Okay. Yeah. That was probably unavoidable. And you told Mickey…"

"I said I knew you were here. I'd seen you out with Pete last night. Pete knew, too. He went for me, then he went over."

Amy nodded slowly, eyes narrowing, nose scrunching, then relaxing. She refocused on Billy. "Okay. You did okay, Billy."

Billy felt a huge weight shift from their chest, and it took a pretty serious act of will to keep their back straight and shoulders up. They didn't even try to do anything about the tears in their eyes.

"The feds aren't coming, are they, Billy?"

"I don't think so."

"Finite Protocol?"

It was an internet legend, but one they both believed in. "I mean, if it hasn't been triggered yet, it'll be any second. Also, Amy, there's nothing on the net. No news, which you'd expect, but nothing on socials, either, not even Twitter or the dark web…"

"Some kind of algorithmic blocking? By the government, or whoever did it?"

"Wouldn't have thought the government has that kind of capability, to be honest, but who knows? Point is…"

"Billy, if you don't get out here, I'm going to kick this fucking door in!"

"Thirty seconds, Bobby!" Billy yelled, then dropped their voice, talking quietly and quickly.

"The point is, it's total fucking chaos out there, and Mickey's got the two Bobbys taking us somewhere off-site, and there's this ridiculously thick fog cutting visibility down to a couple of hundred feet, and…"

"And you think we can grab the stash and go."

Mickey's cash stash. The lockup he thought only he knew about. The one that was located a five minute drive from the tower in a crumbling industrial estate, just one of a row of anonymous, dismal concrete storage garages. The one they'd both talked about for over a year, trying to work out how to get in and out and disappear without being hunted down, inventively tortured, and eventually killed.

"I know we can, Amy. The gang's all here. There's no feds coming. Mickey is totally obsessed with the cases. He'll probably go down for life just for the doors we took this morning, and if we do it right..."

"...he might not even realise the money's gone until he's out!"

Amy grinned. Billy grinned back, then grabbed her hand.

"Let's go, lover," they whispered, then yelled "We're coming, Bobby!"

"'Bout fuckin' time," came the none-too-quiet response.

9:10 am

At fucking last, the kid was making her way towards the checkout. Keith had watched her wheel her trolley for what felt like a million years up and down the same two aisles; plastic girly, and plastic TV tie-in. She'd been hesitant, reaching for toys then snatching her hand back like she'd be caught stealing. It took her seven ball-aching minutes to finally break the spell and start putting toys in her trolley, and even after she'd taken that first step, she continued to take her time; examining the price tags, looking from side to side, muttering to herself, all but screaming guilt and fear. To Keith, the display was equal parts enticing and infuriating, and he'd had to thrust his clenched fists into the pockets of his worn "smart" work trousers to hide the trembling.

Where'd you get that money, honey? He'd thought, over and over again, an idiotic mantra that threatened to obliterate all other mental processing. Where did she get it?

And was there more?

Keith thought there was. A lot more.

And now it was time to find out.

The girl had been all the way at the back of the

cavernous store, and Keith hadn't been sure she was making her way to the till at first, until he clocked her reaching into her jacket pocket, her face flushing as her hand moved inside.

"Hey, kid!"

Keith stood between two aisles, next to the dinosaur bin. He'd picked the location carefully; it was close to the "security office" (really just a room with the CCTV bank, a cleaning closet, and, crucially for Keith in this moment, a fire exit, the alarm for which had been disabled years ago, all the better to allow Keith unfettered access to smoke breaks), and, crucially, it was one of the few camera blind spots in the store.

Can't be too careful, Keith thought, refusing to examine what, exactly, he meant by that thought.

And, oh, how scared she looked! Keith watched her flush to her roots, face stamped with a near-terror that the rising, sickly smile did nothing to disguise. He also got a whiff of cheap perfume, similar to the orange-smelling shit Jenine wore years ago. It was an unsettling association, and Keith gave himself a moment to refocus.

He didn't need to scare her further; the situation, and his uniform, had done their job on that score. *Time for the old Winter charm,* he thought, plastering on his winning grin; the cheeky bloke image that served him so well, hiding his true nature in plain sight.

"It's okay, you're not in trouble! Just need to talk to

you. Can we…?" He gestured at the door marked "Security," wondering if the little shit could even read.

The moment hung, the girl swallowing once, twice, three times, looking to Keith like something four-legged from one of those nature documentaries, interrupted in the act of drinking at the watering hole by some sound or smell.

"The gazelle senses something. She surveys her surroundings, alert for danger. But the Keith-in-the-grass has the perfect camouflage."

Keith laughed. He couldn't help it. He couldn't call the strangled noise the girl made in response an actual giggle, more a cross between a cough and a burp, but he thought her smile looked marginally less strained.

"I think I've got a can of Coke somewhere. Just want to chat. Promise you're not in trouble, okay? Scout's honour!" He held his fingers up in the Cub Scout salute and laughed again. Her reply this time was more like the real thing, but her eyes were still alert, restless, and when he gestured for her to follow him, she did so with slumped shoulders and a pouting bottom lip that looked to Keith like a precursor to tears. "Just leave the trolley outside the office. Don't worry, it'll be safe there, no one's going to nick it from outside Security." Keith reached for the winning grin again, and was gratified to see the girl look up at him with hope as well as fear.

"Will I be able to finish shopping? I mean, after?"

Keith kept the grin in place, widening it just a little.

"Absolutely. Shouldn't take more than five minutes." The lie came as easy as an out breath, and Keith was gratified to see the girl's posture lift a little. "Come on," he said, pushing the door open. The girl took one last look at the contents of the trolley, as if to confirm their reality, then walked through the door into the dimly lit room.

Keith cast one quick glance around the store - all clear - and stepped into the room, pulling the door closed behind him.

The girl had been looking at the black and white security monitors (*fucking kids and screens, fucking disgrace,* Keith thought, reflexively), her nose wrinkling. Keith was so used to the smell of the security room - stale coffee, cheap deodorant, the ghost of an ashtray, and body odour (actually just Keith's smell, bottled up by the tight space and long hours of furtive wanking, *Eau de Keith,* har har) that he barely noticed it, but something about her reaction brought it to the fore of his mind suddenly. He felt a spike of anger at the kid, turning her fucking nose up at a working man, but then her face turned to his and the thought dropped away.

Game on.

"So. I'm Keith. What's your name?"

"Emma." The reply was quiet but clear. Her eyes seemed huge to Keith, watery and weak, and he felt a clench of loathing in his stomach.

110

"Well, Emma, you're not in trouble, yet, but we need to talk about the money. Do you understand?"

A sharp breath in, then silent tears. She nodded, miserable, corners of her mouth turned down, crying freely but quietly. *You knew it wasn't yours. Stupid bitch. You knew something like this would happen.*

"Where'd ya get it?" His voice was cheerful, charming grin as wide as ever, but she started shaking her head, so he added, "Present from Santa, was it?"

He'd intended it as sarcasm, a way to let her know she couldn't bullshit him, that he'd need the truth (*kids lie like breathing, can't help themselves, little shits*), but the impact it had on her was immediate; she stood bolt upright, face draining white, eyes searching Keith's face frantically.

Keith held his peace, kept his smile steady. He had no idea what was going on, but he knew if he held the silence, she'd speak.

She wiped her cheeks, then cuffed the line of clear snot that had been running out of her left nostril, eyes never leaving Keith's. She got her breathing under control. "How did you know?"

Well, now. Keith's mind ran ahead, racing with that scary instinct that had served him so well in his relationships with women and his dealings with men, and his reply came without conscious thought or calculation, sounding as sincere

111

as true love's kiss. "I work for him."

She frowned - not, Keith thought, in disbelief, but honest puzzlement.

He spoke again. "A lot of us do. Toy shops, I mean. Helping with stock. Delivery. That sort of thing."

She nodded, eyes unfocussed, processing what he was saying.

"Yeah, we're all connected to the big guy, this time of year. That's how I knew about the money. In your pocket." He pointed, and her hand reflexively moved to cover it.

Keith laughed. Not a ho-ho-ho, more his pub banter cackle, but it wasn't an unpleasant sound, and his smile was still in place. "It's okay, I mean it, you're not in trouble, it's just…" Keith scratched behind his ear and looked to one side, as though he was embarrassed, "…well, there's been a mistake. You know that, right?"

Direct hit. Her face crumpled, and Keith let it. He'd reached the very end of his improvisational rope, and hoped the storm of emotion she was going through would shake loose what he needed.

She *was* sobbing now, sobbing and nodding, and then she started stuttering, and Keith stood waiting, all the patience in the world, and eventually she stammered out, in a flat low tone of voice "I did know. I should have known. I mean, I did…"

"It's okay, honest mistake." He said this quietly, kindly.

"Why would Santa give me a suitcase full of money? It didn't make sense, but…"

Keith temporarily lost his hearing, blood pounding furiously in his ears, heart feeling like it was punching against his ribcage. By the time he'd got his breathing under control, he heard "…knew I shouldn't have, I'm sorry, am…am I…off the list?"

Keith sunk to his knees, making eye contact, the movement concealing the tremble in his legs that had suddenly developed as adrenaline coursed through his body.

"Listen to me. Listen. It wasn't your mistake, okay?"

"But, I mean, you said…"

"Emma, what day is it?"

Emma frowned, thrown by the question. "Erm…Saturday?"

Keith suppressed a sudden, powerful urge to slap the stupid girl across her face. Instead, keeping his voice even, he said, "Is it Christmas day?"

Emma's frown held, then melted. "Ooooh…Oh, no, of course…"

"Right. It *is* your present, but, well, Santa delivered it early."

"Wow!"

"Wow is right! Big problem! Not your fault, but we can't have people running around with early presents. Especially not big, special presents like this. Messes everything up, you see?"

"Yes! Yes, I get it. Only…" and here, the child looked stricken again, and Keith steeled himself for more waterworks, "…oh, I'm so sorry, but I…The case, the rest of the money, I had to get rid of it." The look of horror on the child's face would, under other circumstances, have been comical, but Keith was experiencing another rush of pounding blood, a negative inversion of his prior euphoria; a sick, sinking feeling.

"Emma. This is really, really important. You need to tell me exactly what you did with the case."

Emma did so, stumbling at first but building confidence through the act of remembering and telling. At the end, she met Keith's eyes. The tears and snot had both started flowing again and to Keith she looked wretched. He couldn't tell what amused/disgusted him more: her trembling fear, or her desperate hope.

He let out a long, deep sigh.

"Well, Emma. We need to get down there as soon as we can. Can you show me the way?"

"Yes, it's not far to walk, we…"

"We're not walking. Every minute counts. My van's

outside. Let's go."

"...Am I in trouble? With Santa?"

"Let's see if the case is still there."

Keith opened the fire escape, looking both ways, grateful he'd managed to get a parking spot so close to the door. He pressed the button on his key fob, and the yellow lights on the back of his red van flashed once.

He gestured for the child to follow him out. Shoulders slumped, she did.

9:15 am

"Where the fuck is my ambulance?!?"

Pointless. The radio was jammed, multiple all-unit calls cutting across each other. Luke clicked the button to keep his own line open and returned his hand to the neck of the injured officer, faintly aware of the smear of warm blood he left across his own cheek as he did so.

He didn't know her. She was a Special. They came and went. Early 30's, he guessed. Wedding band. Luke looked down at his own, the plain gold ring stained with a red so dark it was almost purple.

He shifted his knees to slide them under her back, bring her into more of a sitting up position. The movement caused him to momentarily loosen his grip on her neck wound, and he felt a warm spray of blood against his palm that caused him to cry out involuntarily, a low moan of disgust and despair. He tightened his grip again, leaning forward. "Sorry about that. Just trying to get you more comfortable."

He saw her eyes moving under her lids, and she licked her lips, but didn't respond. Those lips, Luke saw, were developing a bluish tint.

She's fucking dying, man.

Luke looked around him. Within the small circle of visibility the fog offered he could see two additional slumped shapes; both civilians, by the thick winter coats. Unconscious, possibly, but...

It had been over before he arrived. Luke had seen one balaclavaed figure fleeing the scene, a machete hanging from one fist, the other dragging a familiar-looking black wheelie case behind him. Luke had felt a moment of paralysing unreality, mind refusing to process the information his eyes were sending him, then his headlights had picked out the injured officer with the pumping neck wound, and his training kicked in. Report, assess, secure. He brought the car to an emergency stop, conducting an eyeball 360° scan while repeating the officer down call on the radio, hearing without really registering the rise in chatter, ignoring the mumbling from the cuffed man in the back seat.

His field of vision was lousy, but there was no other movement. He assessed the fleeing figure. *Secure casualties first, pursue perpetrators second.* SOP. And whoever it was had seemed keen on getting elsewhere. Still...

He'd climbed out of the car quickly, drawing but not extending his baton, then recovered the first aid kit from the boot. As he'd done so, he'd seen the confiscated black case, and for a second he'd lurched, like the ground was moving under his feet. Then the image of the bleeding officer surfaced, and he slammed the boot, turned, and ran over to the fallen figure.

She was unconscious by the time he reached her, and as Luke saw her breathing slowing and shallowing, he realised that wherever her last words were, they'd already been spoken. The thought carried no apparent weight, but Luke was suddenly aware of a tiredness that he normally only felt at the end of a double overnight shift - or when things were bad with Rob, of course. His eyes burned, the coldness of the air and the unreal dull aura of the fog feeling abrasive, and he was aware of a numbness creeping into his feet, his kneeling position cutting off circulation. He thought about trying to move, remembered the neck wound, looked down, then quickly looked away. He'd hold her while she passed, he could do that much, but, he discovered, he'd really rather not watch.

He tried to listen to the radio while scanning the oppressively close horizon, willing one of the slumped figures on the ground to move, some of the distant sirens to come closer. It was impossible to make out individual messages; but the fragments he could hear suggested there had been attacks on queues of people outside pretty much every bank, building society, and post office in the city, all in the last fifteen minutes. Luke was aware of one nearby estate gang whose weapon of choice was machetes, but they didn't have the numbers to hit a bunch of locations at once.

And why were civilians lining up outside banks a couple of days before Christmas to be mugged, for fuck's sake?

But Luke thought he knew.

The cases.

It made no sense, but neither did the carnage he was hearing right now, via snatches of intelligible chatter in a rising babble of overlapping voices; gangs or individuals committing door-to-door burglaries with menace, break-ins, a body thrown off a balcony in Melrose Towers (*that's pretty close to home*)…he thought again about the fleeing figure, the case he'd been pulling. The visibility was too poor to be certain, but…

Fuck that. You know what you saw.

Luke started running Henry's story through his head, trying to recall the ancient past of fifteen minutes ago, when the world was at least pretending to make some kind of sense. *He'd found it under his tent when he woke up…*

"…03, repeat, 403, Peartree Bridge, missing child is white female…."

Luke felt his stomach lurch. The crosstalk overwhelmed the report, and he leaned his head towards the radio, closing his eyes, trying to tune out the noise, find the signal.

"…years old, Emma…"

The crosstalk rose again, and this time, the

hammering of Luke's heart in his ears made it impossible for him to filter it out; he could hear the tone of the dispatcher's voice but couldn't make out a single word.

Still, he'd heard enough.

Emma.

Should have been Syd, of course. Syd Danger, what a fucking name, Luke and Rob Danger's little girl. *His* girl. His DNA, his seed, but the surrogate had backed out, courts had backed her, Luke's own biological paternity not counting for shit, and thanks to Rob's instability…

Luke closed his eyes, took a deep breath, tried desperately to focus.

You don't know it's her. Didn't get the age. Emma could be the mother. Plenty of young families on Peartree.

All true. But his stomach was a cold ball of lead, and his breathing was becoming a pant, in spite of his attempts to keep it slow. Too many thoughts, crowding in. The girl he'd kept careful, discrete tabs on, the agony of learning about the mother's lifestyle, the trip to the shelter thanks to the aggro boyfriend, the fucking drugs and the support worker (nothing he could act on, because of the fucking court order; information he wasn't supposed to have) Rob slipping further and further away into depression; Major, Luke's retired partner from his K9 unit days, a brilliant dog but a lousy substitute for a child, the miserable shitshow his life had somehow slid into, year by painful year, and now…

He opened his eyes. The glassy eyes of the dead woman stared back at him, seeming almost to gleam in the sheet white of her face.

Luke gently lifted her head from his lap, placed it on the tarmac, then stood, both knees popping with the effort. He felt tingly warmth creep down his legs as blood started flowing back to his feet; ordinarily a sensation he'd find distracting to the point of anger; now merely something he noted, then moved on from.

It is her. And even if it isn't…

Even if it isn't, it's a kid missing in this insanity, and nobody else is going to give a shit.

And, Luke discovered, that was more than enough for him.

"Control, this is Victor 2-4."

No response. Then, suddenly, the chatter cut out altogether. The babble of voices had been such a constant companion for the last few minutes that the silence hit Luke hard, causing him to shiver. He waited a few precious seconds, then started to walk back towards his car, absentmindedly wiping his blood-caked hand on his trousers.

"Control, this is Victor 2-4, respond."

Nothing.

What fresh fuckery is this?

Luke opened the driver's side door and sat, legs stretched out into the street. He noted with no real surprise that the sirens he'd been able to hear in the distance had cut off. Could just be out of range, but Luke didn't think so.

He turned in his seat and looked at Henry. Henry looked back. Luke could see the man was freaked, but he held his gaze steadily enough.

Luke sighed.

"Going to have to cut you loose, Henry."

"Come again, mate?"

Luke had to admire Henry's delivery, considering the circumstances. And it was a fair question.

"Special end of the world deal, Henry. Petty shit no longer holds any priority."

"What…?"

But Luke was already on the move, opening the passenger door, pulling Henry out of the car, turning him around, uncuffing him, then quickly backing off, baton back in his fist, still retracted, for now.

Henry rubbed his wrists as he turned around. Luke saw his face and let himself breathe a little calmer. He saw fear, confusion, but no aggression.

"I'm free to go?"

Luke nodded, gestured towards the fog. "Yup. No charges, no further questions. I'd say don't leave town, but I doubt like hell any services are running."

Henry frowned. Opened his mouth. Closed it. Luke sighed. "Out with it, mate."

"Can…can I get the case back?"

Luke looked at Henry, momentarily baffled beyond the powers of speech. *Did he really just…?* Henry licked his lips. His frown deepened, but he didn't look away.

Luke looked up into the grey sky and laughed. He hadn't meant to, but the sound came out of him, startling both men a little. Then he held up his bloody hand. "The men who did this had machetes. The guy I saw fleeing the scene was dragging a case. Just like yours. You want to take your chances out there? Really?"

Henry winced, but he didn't look away, and Luke realised Henry did indeed fancy his chances…or was willing to take the risk. The realisation hit Luke's stomach like a gut punch, nausea rising first, then a tidal anger that felt close to overwhelming. The pale face of the dead Special floated up in his mind. *Going to have to save this idiot from himself, fuck me.* Luke flicked his wrist, baton deploying beside his leg, and stalked towards Henry. He barely recognised the bellow that tore from his throat as his own.

"Get the fuck out of here, you fucking clown! I'll fucking end you right here!"

Henry flinched, then, realising he'd not yet been

attacked, turned and fled.

Luke watched him get swallowed by the fog, then slumped back into his car seat. He tried the radio one more time but got no response.

You know what that means.

He did. It meant that, if he headed out to Peartree to look for Emma, he'd be committing the instantly sackable offence of dereliction of duty, with the very real possibility of jail time thrown in.

Assuming it hasn't all come crashing down, of course.

Luke was fairly sure it hadn't, though, and wouldn't. If he was even close to right - if cases stuffed full of money had just appeared randomly at some point overnight - things would get rough for a while, and they'd need to deploy The Finite Protocol until things *were* back under control, but...

But they will. And when they do...

Luke closed his hands into fists. *Fuck it. Don't care.* It was a lie, but it got him back under control. He caught his eye in the rearview mirror. He saw fear, but also anger. The anger looked stronger.

Let's fucking do it, he thought, then turned the ignition key.

His inside pocket started vibrating, the muffled tones of the opening bars of *Mr. Brightside* ringing out.

"Fuck!"

Luke dug under his stab vest and pulled out his phone, caller ID confirming what he already knew: Rob.

"Rob. You okay?"

He tried to keep his voice businesslike. Rob had agreed that, when Luke was on duty, he'd only call in a genuine emergency. As far as Rob knew, Luke was riding shotgun with Steve the dick, and Rob further knew that meant Luke would have to be circumspect; sure, none of them were supposed to have their personal phones on them, and sure, they all flouted that rule and turned blind eyes where needed, but...

"Luke! Luke, thank God!"

Luke's free hand tightened its grip on the steering wheel, then reached over his shoulder and pulled his seatbelt into place on autopilot. The fear in Rob's voice was unmistakable. Luke felt himself go cold.

"Rob, what..."

"They're trying to get in! Oh, God, Luke, they're smashing the windows! Major...!'

The line cut off dead. Luke held the phone away from his ear.

No service.

The radio gave a short burst of static, then a robot voice cut in. "Finite Protocol initiated. Return immediately to muster point. Repeat, Finite Protocol initiated. Return immediately..."

Luke shut the radio off. On the nearby grid road, an engine noise resolved into the shape of a red van, revving pretty hard (*got to be doing forty in a thirty,* Luke's cop brain fired on automatic, *but, today, so fucking what?).* The vehicle appeared briefly, then the fog swallowed it. Otherwise, the city centre was eerily quiet.

What the fuck do I do now? he thought. But one look in the mirror and he knew the answer to that.

He revved the car, thought for a moment, turned on the flashing lights. *Leave the siren, though. Don't want any other coppers to hear me.*

In that moment, Luke gave up being an officer of the law. He pulled out of the car park fast, already mentally mapping the quickest route to his destination, leaving his old life behind him in a cloud of petrol fumes.

9:20 am

"Open the back, Billy." Bobby D barked the order, already half out of the van. Billy locked eyes with Amy for a second, enjoying the way the corner of her mouth twitched in amusement, then said, "Sure." As they opened up the back doors of Bobby D's legendary white van (hypothetically used as transport for the Two Bobbies' largely theoretical painting and decorating business, but primarily used for the transportation of stolen goods) and climbed out, Billy took in their surroundings. The garden centre was just off the dual carriageway, close enough that even with the fog Billy could see to the central reservation. Very little traffic, which struck Billy as odd for a road that was a major artery feeding the city centre, last Sunday before Christmas. The fog would discourage some, they supposed, but…

"Come on, no time for daydreaming, giz a fuckin' hand," growled Bobby B, shoving Billy to one side with a grunt of effort before tossing something into the rear of the van, the suspension protesting with the impact.

Billy took in the five-kilo sack of "10mm Driveway Gravel", then Bobby B, already heading back to the display pile outside the store, passed Bobby D sauntering towards the van with another sack over his shoulder.

Okay.

Billy walked over to the pile and grabbed one. They debated taking one over each shoulder but decided that might be seen as showing off; worse, might give away useful information Bobbies B and D didn't need concerning Billy's physical strength. Instead, they took one sack, gripping it awkwardly to their stomach and making a point of puffing as they duckwalked it back to the van. Piling their load in on top of the two sacks already there, Billy saw the van was already sitting lower at the rear. *Our gas mileage is going to be for shit,* they thought. They looked over at Amy, staring back at them from the jury-rigged seat the Bobbies had built for anyone insane enough to want to travel in the back of the white transit van o' larceny. She held up her phone and mouthed something, but Billy couldn't make out what.

They started to reach for their own phone - a reflex - then forced themselves to stop. They had a job to do, Mickey's orders no less powerful for coming via the two Bobbies, and now was not the time to be seen as less than a good soldier. Billy returned to the pile.

Two more trips (Amy tried once more to communicate with Billy, then rolled her eyes and turned around, opening up some match 3 game with primary colours and highly irritating sound effects) and Bobby B put his hand on Billy's shoulder as they turned back.

"That'll do, Billy. Best not push our luck, the arse is dragging enough as it is." Billy nodded, relieved, but also puzzled, and frustrated by their puzzlement. Why the fuck were they stealing sacks of gravel, this morning of all mornings?

Bobby B moved to the passenger side as Bobby D lowered his significant frame into the driver's seat. Billy rejoined Amy in the back, slamming the rear doors closed. Distracted and anxious as they were, they found her proximity both soothing and intoxicating; a smell that was part soap, part cheap underarm deodorant, but with something sweet underneath Billy thought of as just *her*.

Billy turned their head and risked a smile, there and gone. She didn't respond, but instead flashed her phone screen towards them. It displayed a single word.

FINITE

Billy felt their heart rate pick up and pulled out their phone.

No signal.

Billy checked 4G was on. Nothing there, either. Billy flicked through half a dozen open tabs, hitting the refresh button. Disconnection messages flashed up.

Fuck. It's really happening.

What did it mean?

No cops, that was number one. Likely no blue lights at all. *Bad day to be in a fire. Or a car accident, for that matter.*

Would they close the motorways? If they did, would they enforce the closure? Billy thought not, except maybe with cameras; in any case, it shouldn't matter; the authorities wouldn't be looking for either Billy or Amy, and Mickey had basically no reach outside of MK3. Whatever the status of these new notes (Billy still thought it most likely the people in charge would be able to identify the new money via the serial numbers, eventually), Mickey's lockup stash cash was untraceable - not least because Mickey could never, ever report it missing.

And what about Mickey's security?

The thing was, the man understood that the most valuable part of the lockup was the anonymity. Only a very small number of people in the crew knew it existed, and none apart from Mickey (and, more recently, Billy and Amy) knew where it was. Close, but off the main roads. Not much traffic. The only other business nearby was "Dodgy" Del's Motors, the place you went to if you needed an MOT certificate for your deathtrap white van, or if you'd gotten hold of a car that wasn't, strictly speaking, yours, and you wanted to convert it into a small amount of quid so Del could convert it into a large amount of parts. In short, it was a good spot. Mickey understood the more visible security, the more you were screaming "Rob me!"

The unit lock looked robust, but Billy had picked the same model many, many times, practising in their flat. Amy wasn't a bad lockpick, but Billy had a natural gift bordering on the spooky. She could get them inside in five minutes, Billy in less than one.

The silent alarm should have been trickier, but Mickey had gotten sloppy; the last time he'd visited the lockup, observed by Billy and Amy via a discreet webcam rigged to a lamppost across the street, he'd not blocked the view of the keypad code. The number he'd punched in - 2011 - was a combination of the day of his birth and the day of Amy's. It could be a coincidence, the code should change every few weeks…but the rig looked old to Billy, and the speed and nonchalance with which Mickey typed in the number, along with the significance of it, suggested the code hadn't changed in years, if at all. In fact, Billy would lay money the same 4 digits would be the pin on Mickey's phone and bank card - if Mickey even *had* a bank card.

Which only left Mickey's webcam. They'd been sweating that for months, trying to figure out a way to either hack or spoof the signal. The best idea they'd come up with was to take a photo from just above the camera's position, then slide it over the lens. It might work, but getting in to take the picture was a challenge, as was knowing the time of day it'd need taking, to make sure it matched. Plus, there was no guarantee it would work; if the cam output was being monitored closely in real time, the subterfuge would immediately be spotted. And Billy thought it probably was.

Or had been. With the networks down…And would Mickey have thought to put someone he trusted on the site directly? With the chaos he was at the centre of, would he even know the network was down, or understand what it meant?

Billy thought not. Billy thought this was the chance Amy and they had been waiting for.

Billy hugged their laptop bag close to their chest reflexively. That was definitely one of the perks of being known as the Geek Squad, Billy reflected; no one questioned why you always carried a bag.

There *was* a laptop in there, fully charged and with some browsers set up with certain protocols that Billy thought *might* be able to circumvent whatever big switch the government had just thrown, should they need it (to contact their *real* crew, for example, not that they had the slightest intention of doing so), but the real gold was the two fake passports and driving licences sewn into the cable pocket.

Months of planning. All it took was the end of the world.

As Bobby D slammed the van into reverse, the engine protesting the extra weight in the back, Billy stole a glance at

Amy. She was back to her match three game, but Billy saw a small smile, there and gone, that they knew was meant for them.

It's going to be okay, thought Billy.

Then Bobby D pulled out onto the dual carriageway, accelerating hard. The roar of the engine, under strain from a boot full of gravel, masked the sound of the red van barrelling down the road towards them. The first they knew of it was when the headlights finally pierced the fog, turning Bobby B's side of the car into glaring daylight.

And by then it was too late.

9:25 am

He'd been sweating the copper behind him, running blues and gaining, so when Keith brought his eyes from the rearview to the road, the white van was just fucking *there*. Keith moaned, already slamming his feet down on the brake and clutch, dragging the wheel hard left. The kid's screams were almost drowned by the tyres; a hellish symphony. Keith saw it all with unasked-for clarity; the strobing blue and red from behind that had drawn his eyes from the road in the first place, flashing in the rearview, the white shitbox, effectively stationary, nose just beginning to turn away. His own van starting to slide to the left.

Too fast. Too slow. Too late.

The impact of the collision slammed Keith into the driver's side door. His head cracked off the window, and for a precious second, the colour drained out of his world. The girl fucking howled. Pain and fear. Shrieking. Keith's grip held but his foot slipped off the brake, causing the van to lurch further to the left, nose crossing the grass of the central reservation.

For a second Keith felt suspended in time, almost

floating. The van was facing a bus stop on the other side of the road. He had time to realise that he needed to turn the other way, now, or he'd likely skid across the damp grass until he was facing oncoming traffic. He sent the signal to his arms, mind moving far faster than his muscles - *go, go, fucking go* - and the wheel turned under his white-knuckled fists. He started to lift his foot to regain the pedals.

He thought *I've fucking got this.*

Then the police car hit him in the back.

It was a glancing blow, but it pushed the van forward, and his foot came slamming back down on the accelerator. The van straightened up and felt to Keith like it *leapt* towards the bus stop, a dog after a chew toy. His face broke into a terrified grin - *fuck my luck* - and he wrenched the wheel right, but it was a futile effort; he'd miss the bus stop, but they were clearly going off the road.

As the van hit the gap between the bus stop and the crash barrier, Keith finally remembered to take his foot off the gas. They crested a small rise, and for a moment, hanging suspended over the drop, Keith could see nothing but the grey horizon of fog, suffused with hazy light from an invisible sun.

His stomach turned as the van dipped forward. A row of recently planted saplings filled his field of vision. He yelled, slammed on the brakes, tried to turn a steering wheel that suddenly felt set in concrete. Then he threw his arms in front

of his face.

There were a series of crashes, splintering noises. Keith felt his arms peppered with what felt like pebbles. *Safety glass,* he thought. Then another sudden collision threw him forward, seatbelt locking and cutting off air, his face, party cushioned by his arms, colliding with the steering wheel. The van began to spin, still falling, sliding, *don't tip, please don't tip, please,* then what felt like an explosion, pinning Keith's arms to his face, crushing his nose.

He opened his eyes. Couldn't see anything. He blinked, felt fabric against his eyelids.

The van was still sliding, *don't tip, please don't,* but they hit something solid on the rear left side which sent the van tilting the other way, then Keith felt the centre of gravity shift, drew in a sharp, painful breath…

The noise was deafening as the van began to roll; metal slamming and glass shattering. The belt and whatever had Keith's arms trapped pinned him tight, but he could feel each impact the entire length of his spine, and suddenly he could also taste blood.

Gonna fucking die. Fuck me.

Suddenly, the jolting stopped, and they were just falling and spinning.

Keith screwed his eyes shut and hoped for a quick and painless death.

The final crash made the other knocks feel like love taps; the impact forced all the air out of Keith's lungs, and his spine felt briefly like a single splinter of bone, locked rigid and sending bolts of pain into his skull and down his limbs, hard enough that he imagined he was feeling something - several somethings, actually - slamming together hard enough to break.

The van had stopped moving. Keith held his breath.

The silence was so total that for a moment Keith thought he'd been deafened; that some combination of the hellish noise of the van's descent and that final impact had burst his eardrums, or possibly shattered the small bones that, he vaguely remembered from school, transmitted sound to his brain.

Then he heard a sob.

The sound came from his left-hand side. Reflexively, he tried to turn his head, but he couldn't; whatever was pinning his arms to his face still had him, arms pushing his face, head jammed against the backrest of his seat.

Okay.

Slowly, carefully, he let out his held breath. Muscles in his back complained at the movement, but only twinges, and his chest seemed okay. He registered that he *was* sitting in the seat, not just held in by the seat belt; the van had landed on its wheels. *Won't have done much for my suspension,* he thought, too distracted to register the joke. Inhaling slowly, the stale coffee smell of his jacket sleeve coating the inside of his nose, Keith wiggled his toes, then flexed his feet. They moved easily. He lifted his knees. They also moved, though his back sent another twinge.

Okay. Still in the game. Not a spinal case, no broken ribs, somehow...

And was it his imagination, or had the pressure on his face eased a little? He pushed forward with his arms.

That *did* hurt. He experienced a moment of elation, then stabbing pains in both shoulders, deep and strong enough that his breath came out in a forced rush, sweat popping across his forehead and shoulders. He growled, frustration and pain, teeth gritted together.

Next to him, he heard the unmistakable sound of a seatbelt being unbuckled.

Fuck. He pushed again, harder, the pain rising, feeling like a burning brand across his shoulder now, spreading up his neck, but there was more give, and suddenly he could see light, praise the Lord. He turned his head to the left - more pain, shooting up his neck, into his skull, forcing tears into his eyes.

His view was still partly obscured by his arm and the tears, but he could see the blurred figure of the girl, wriggling in her seat. He blinked furiously to clear his eye, feeling a tear roll down his cheek.

"Hey," he tried to say, but all that came out was a dry croak that turned into a cough, and suddenly his back was fucking agony, on fire, and his jaw clicked shut, teeth pushing hard enough that he felt something grinding in his jaw muscles, but that felt like news being beamed in from a distant galaxy next to the rod of molten lava that had apparently replaced his spine. He closed his eyes, held his breath, and willed himself to be still.

The tickle in his throat felt like something solid; like he had a twig, or possibly an entire fucking sapling lodged in there, but he ground his teeth and held his breath and *would not* cough, and gradually the pain subsided to a dull ache he didn't trust at all. His mouth was full of saliva and his whole body felt like it had been dipped in sweat. He took a few shallow, panting breaths, then swallowed. For a second, he thought he would gag, but he screwed his eyes up and willed his stomach to settle, and, little by little, it did. His throat still felt tender and infuriatingly tickly, but the worst of the danger seemed to have passed.

He opened his eyes. His arms were no longer pinned to his face but suspended a couple of inches in front of it, and behind them he could see the sheer white of the slowly deflating airbag. There was a small smear of bright red blood, from where he'd bitten his lip as the van had started rolling.

There were more noises from the seat next to him,

and he came dangerously close to turning his head before the memory of his recent agony came surging up. *Fuck me, old habits,* he thought, swivelling his eyes instead.

The angle was bad enough that his vision was doubled, his right eye only seeing the far edge of the girl, but it was enough to see that the kid was on the move. Her arm was free of the seatbelt and she'd started wrestling with her door. *Good luck, kid,* Keith thought - judging by the buckled frame, the door wouldn't open even if the fucking Hulk was doing the tugging.

"I *know!*" she said, looking out of the passenger window. As though there was someone standing there that she was talking to. Keith felt a prickle of unease across his scalp and shifted his eyes briefly.

Nothing.

Back to the girl. She was pale, almost milk-white, a single thin scratch across her right cheek, but other than that, she looked unharmed.

Keith almost cleared his throat, remembered the cough, stopped himself, swallowed once more, then "Know what, Emma?"

At the gravelly croak of his voice, her head snapped back around (the movement made Keith wince, though it didn't seem to cause her any pain), and Keith saw that she wasn't just, or even mainly, scared; she was *furious.*

"You're a bad man! Rachel said and I didn't listen! And now..."

Keith shook his head, felt the tears welling up, but his throat was raw, couldn't trust himself to speak. Instead, he started to slide his arm slowly towards the seatbelt release. She caught the movement, gasped, then stood on her seat, wriggling through the windscreen, sleeves of her coat pulled up around her hands. *No you don't,* thought Keith, but as he hit the seatbelt release button the sudden movement sent a wave of pain across his shoulders which pushed the breath from his body. He let his arms hang, panting, eyes following the girl wriggling down the bonnet of the van. There was a crunch as her feet landed on the gravel.

"Don't!" It was meant to come out calm, pleading - *What about Santa?* - but the crash had robbed his voice of all its smoothness, and the harsh bark of the word seemed only to further inflame her. She glared at Keith - *so much hate, for one so young* - and said, "You're a bad man! She tried to tell me!"

"I'm not a..."

"You are! You are, and I'm telling on *you!*"

The words were ridiculous, and Keith forced himself to try to smile, but he felt something very cold in his stomach. *Fuckin' snitch, is it?*

"What about...?"

But she'd already turned away, hands over her ears;

and, walking with only a slight limp, was quickly claimed by the fog.

> *Well.*

> *This is a bit of a fucking mess.*

9:30 am

Luke ran, taking care not to push; maintaining the mile-eating pace he'd developed over the last few years, all those early morning and post-shift visits to the gym to get rid of or gear up for the stress of the day. *And to avoid having to spend too much time with Rob, let's not forget that,* an angry voice in his mind reminded him, yeah, sure, okay, that, too.

Luke tried to focus on his breathing, the feeling of his legs impacting with the ground, the crunching of the redway gravel under his work boots. The uniform was bulky, and the shoulder bag from the boot of his car kept an unwelcome percussive rhythm against his right leg, but even so, Luke felt confident he could maintain his current pace for a good half an hour; twice what he'd need to get home.

He replayed the accident as his feet covered ground; the red van that had sped up in front of him instead of just getting out the way (convinced the lights were for him, Luke supposed, though why the fuck the driver would think that was a mystery he imagined he'd never solve) before taking a sudden evasive action that made it slow down. Luke had seen the hazard for himself a moment later, and, already braking, managed to swerve to avoid the white van, but in doing so, he'd rear ended the red van. He'd felt the jolt of the impact all the way up his spine, and his own car had ground to a halt in the central reservation. Adrenaline surging, Luke had checked himself for injuries, hearing the red van crashing and rolling, observing the white van (*Ford, reg LV59 6JS,* his cop mind recorded automatically) speeding away from the scene, a nasty crimp in the passenger side door.

Keen to get the fuck away from an RTA (*is everyone on the road right now engaged in something nefarious?* Luke asked himself, and he'd meant it as a joke but as he'd thought about it, he wasn't so sure it was). He went to try starting his car, but the smell of petrol froze his hand on the way to the ignition, and instead, he'd grabbed his kit bag from the boot, locked up the vehicle in what he realised was almost certainly a futile gesture, and crossed the road to join up with the redway, already setting his jogger's pace.

He had to get home.

He reached a junction and turned right, keeping parallel with the grid road that ran most of the way to his estate. An impulse had him checking for Melrose Tower on the horizon, though the fog was still so thick he couldn't even see the next streetlamp. He thought about how the tip of the tower's shadow would fall over the back of his garden on a long summer night.

His garden. Rob's garden, really. He did all the work; Luke just enjoyed sitting out there with a beer when the weather was good. Rob said it was good for him, helped him relax, get some perspective when things were tough.

About that, Luke was less sure.

The rhythm of running brought back The Speech. Luke had been prepping it for close to five years now, working, reworking, perfecting, cutting, adding, shaping. It had started out purely as a way to process his feelings after …

What could he call it? He and Rob didn't fight, or row, because Rob…wouldn't. Maybe couldn't. When there was a disagreement, or when Luke's frustrations boiled over, Rob would just go quiet. Sometimes leave the room, sometimes just hug himself and wait for Luke to stop. Often there would be tears. It was completely impossible for Luke to manage; whatever his frustration with Rob's behaviour, his inability to do things he said he was going to, his fucking endless misery, it would crash against that silence and Luke would feel his anger draining away, replaced by a dull, aching despair.

And then, increasingly, Luke would head to the gym.

It was tempting to blame the failure of the surrogacy for Rob's state, and of course it hadn't helped…but Rob's problems predated that - in point of fact, had been part of what the mother's barrister had used to make the custody argument - a fact that Luke found indigestible, impossible to talk about with anyone. How could he? *Who* could he? It would have felt disloyal. And anyway, Luke loved Rob.

Had loved Rob.

The slow motion drain of that feeling, as Rob's mental health ebbed and flowed, the odd good day, sure, but many more bad days, and far too many fucking *flat,* listless days, the failure of the surrogacy an inflection point, a sheer drop that Rob had never come all the way back from, and the hell of it was, Luke knew it wasn't what Rob wanted, knew it wasn't his fault…

But it's not mine either, Luke thought, jaw clenched.

And that's where The Speech began.

It was a well-worn fantasy, words Luke would never, could never, bring himself to say, and it burned all the brighter for it; an escape hatch he'd never open, to a freedom he'd never be able to enjoy because of the guilt he'd feel for getting there, and was there ever a more poisonous chalice, a more vicious trap, than love?

Luke thought there was not. And though he could admit to himself he no longer loved his husband, he also knew Rob adored him; that he was, in fact, Rob's only real anchor to the world. Without him…

Luke couldn't do that. Not to the man he'd once promised to be true to until the end.

So, instead, as his feet carried him further from the home of his daughter to his damaged, unhappy husband (that at least some of Rob's unhappiness might stem from an understanding on some level that Luke no longer loved him was a notion that would not have occurred to Luke in a million years, and probably wouldn't have helped if it had), Luke ran through The Speech once more in his mind.

Rob. Listen. I love you. But things have to change. I need a change...

The scene unfolded behind his eyes as the yards passed under his feet.

9:35 am

Mickey was stood inside the laundrette, beside a pile of black suitcases. As Billy and Bobby D stood waiting for Mickey to speak, Keef pushed his way in, dragging in two more cases that he stacked neatly with the others. Billy did a quick count and made at least fifty; more than they'd expected from the towers, given their own hit rate on the 14th floor. The shiny black surfaces reflected back the fluorescent strip lighting brightly enough to make Billy wish they hadn't left their sunnies back in their flat.

Had that really been this morning?

Billy looked the room over as Amy retreated to the back wall, hoisting herself up onto one of the dryers. All the washing machine doors were open, and the change machine and gambler had both been jimmied, spilling out coins onto the floor. There was a pile of blue plastic crates in the corner - the kind with the hinged lids that fold over from each side. All were currently open and stacked.

They were identical to the crates Billy had glimpsed inside Mickey's lockup.

Next to Amy were a couple of automated cash

counters and a large ball of rubber bands.

Interesting.

"Where the fuck ya been, lads and Billy?" Mickey was wearing the fixed grin, not his real one. Billy sometimes thought of this as his we-are-not-amused grin, which was kinda ridiculous, but it fit.

Bobby D glared at Billy - *shut the fuck up, you* - and replied, "Visibility's for shit. Had a near miss coming out of the garden centre. Slowed us down."

"Near miss, was it?" Mickey shifted his gaze between Billy and Bobby D, as Bobby B huffed his way through the door and dumped a sack of gravel in the corner. The look of put-upon disgust he threw Bobby D and Billy before heading back out was comical, but Billy didn't feel much like laughing.

Mickey let the silence hang as he continued to shift his eye contact, slowly, deliberately. Bobby D was likely already sweating. Billy remained calm, but they were on high alert, ready for an explosion of temper, considering possible reactions, defensive and otherwise. Amy's presence reduced the chance of violence but didn't eliminate it; weighed against that was the fact that Mickey looked as wired as Billy had ever seen him. *I'm not the only one who sees today as their golden ticket.*

Eventually, Mickey spoke, looking at Billy but talking to Bobby, another mind game Mickey often deployed to good effect. They stayed calm, keeping their face carefully neutral.

"And why do I get the impression that if I ask Billy here what the score is, I'll get a different reply? Huh?"

On the last word, he shifted his gaze back to Bobby, and Billy chanced a glance in the other man's direction.

Bobby D was a sweaty mess, licking his lips, hand trembling as he pushed his fringe back from his eyes. *If I were a judge, I'd find you guilty,* thought Billy, and a look back at Mickey showed a similar notion was crossing his mind.

Billy kept still, kept quiet. They'd not been asked to speak, and it would be a mistake to.

After a couple of excruciating seconds, Bobby cracked. "Oh, yeah, no, I hadn't finished! I mean, yeah, well, near miss, we got clipped, red van, passenger side's a bit of a mess..."

"So, that'd be 'near miss' in the sense of 'actual RTA', then?"

"Yeah, well, no, I mean it was a near miss because we could have gotten really banged up, you know, not made it back, sort of thing..."

"I see. So you had a near miss that was actually a collision with another vehicle, and that's why you're late?"

Mickey had turned all his attention to Bobby, and so did Billy, willing him to keep his mouth shut, leave it there. It was clear to Billy that Mickey's paranoia and aggression levels were seriously amped, and whilst wound-up Mickey was, potentially, stupid Mickey, paranoid Mickey could be a pretty serious problem for anyone planning to, say, rob the man of all the street cash in his lockup.

Bobby glanced quickly at Billy. Mickey saw it and quickly closed with Bobby, that scary-fast stride that fucked with people's fight or flight; too fast to outrun, but no actual attack to defend against. "Don't look at them! Look at me! What else, knobhead?"

"Yeah, no, I was saying…"

"Fucking say, then!" Spit from Mickey's mouth sprayed Bobby's face. Bobby flinched, then started talking fast, stammering.

"There was a rozzer! Running blues, like it was chasing the other van, I dunno, maybe not, it all happened fast, but the van hit us, then the copper hit the other van and ended up in the central reservation grass. We got out of there quick, but it looked pretty banged up to me, don't think it could have followed even if it'd wanted to…"

Mickey slapped Bobby. The sound was like a rifle crack, and Billy saw a red mark rising on Bobby's right cheek. Bobby's eye filled with water, but he held Mickey's glare, which Billy thought was a smart move.

"And you wasn't going to tell me?"

"No, Mickey…!"

The second slap landed on the other cheek. Bobby

looked like he was crying, though his breathing was steady. His Adam's apple bobbed up and down under the stubble on his neck.

"Do. Not." Mickey's voice was quiet. Almost a purr. "Don't. No more bullshit, you're shit at it and it's a bad day to not be telling me everything."

Bobby drew breath, opened his mouth as if to speak, closed it again. Mickey nodded.

"Good." Holding Bobby's gaze, still close enough for one of his patented nose-cracking headbutts, Mickey called out, "It's as he said, Billy?"

"Yeah," Billy answered immediately, forcing themself to keep their voice calm, even, slow. "The cop was battered, front smashed in and smoking. Didn't see it move before we were out of sight. No blues or sirens the rest of the way."

"Any chance he made Bobby's van?"

Billy had anticipated the question, and the lie came out smooth. "There's always a chance, but I'd be surprised. He was facing the wrong way, we got up to speed pretty fast, and with the fog…" They shrugged, but Mickey still wasn't looking their way. Instead he was glaring at Bobby.

Billy ran the story through in their head. Could either Bobby contradict it? They thought not. They'd both seemed preoccupied with yelling at each other about the collision, the need to get the fuck away. If either of them *had* looked in the rearview, they'd have seen what Billy saw; the cop car pointed damn near directly at them. But Billy didn't think they had, and they thought it was worth the risk to try and lower Mickey's fear of the law putting a premature end to his crime of the century.

"No other blues?" Mickey hadn't turned his head, but Billy knew the comment was meant for them.

"Not a peep, Mickey. Bit fucking weird, how quiet it is."

Mickey's riveted-on grin dissolved into his real one, and Billy felt a surge of relief they held tight, keeping their face and body still.

"Well, it's a nutty day, innit? Probably got lots on. Like us!"

Bobby B dropped another sack of gravel on the pile and turned to leave.

"That'll do, pig, that'll do," said Mickey, chuckling. The look of relief on Bobby B's face struck Billy as so comic they had to work hard to suppress a smile.

"That's a fuckload of gravel," Bobby said, mopping his sweaty brow with the sleeve of his black puffer jacket.

"Yeah, well, it's a fuckload of money, innit?"

What the fuck are you up to, you maniac?

"What's the plan, boss?" It was Bobby B, and Billy could have kissed him.

Mickey looked at Billy and tipped him a wink, like they were in on something. More fucking mind games. Billy nodded slightly, acknowledging the gesture.

"Ain't you ever heard of money laundering?"

All of a sudden, Billy *did* get it, and this time, they did nothing to suppress the smile.

He's almost *as clever as he is greedy.*

Billy allowed their mind to wander a little as Mickey talked through the process; a small cup load of gravel in each drum, then as much cash as possible - "tear the tape and bung 'em in, we'll bundle them back up after", gesturing at the counters. Run the shortest cycle, a ten minute spin. Take the laundered notes (actually, dirtied, but Billy understood the point) over to the counters, 5K bundles. Load them into the crates. Make the new money look like old money. Even if the authorities were able to trace the new cash using serial numbers, Mickey's 'laundered' cash would almost certainly be good enough for street deals. Which was, after all, Mickey's bread and butter.

This might actually work, Billy thought, with admiration and just a little horror.

"I want every drum turning until the cases are empty. It's going to make a massive din, so wear ear plugs or something, all right, Amy?" She didn't acknowledge the comment, but dug a pair of earbuds from her jacket pocket and put them in. Billy patted their laptop case, feeling the comforting shape of their noise cancelling headphones.

"And I want it doing yesterday, understand? Sooner the cash is out of here, the better."

So he's going to stash this lot in the lockup with the rest of his cash. Smart. Yes, and also, just a bit of a total pain in the arse. Billy thought about the number of cases, counted up the number of open drums - twenty-four - and wondered if they had even an hour before Mickey made his first deposit. They could wait until after that first run (might even be smarter, give Mickey less chance to realise the money was missing) but Billy's gut was telling them very strongly that the sooner Amy and they could get the fuck out of MK, the better their chances were.

Well, nobody said it was going to be easy.

Bobby B's question broke across Billy's thoughts. "It's a lot of work, boss. Any chance of the others mucking in?"

"None, Bobby. They're out hunting and gathering."

Billy looked back at the pile of cases. A lot to have come out of the tower, yes. But if Mickey was expanding the operation to the rest of the immediate neighbourhood…

Oh, Amy, love, we really need to get out of here, Billy thought. They immediately set their mind to figuring out how.

9:40 am

Keith's shoulders and neck were finally settling to a dull ache. He'd found an ancient box of ibuprofen in his glove box and dry swallowed six before climbing through the windscreen and finally setting foot back on solid ground, so he guessed they were finally kicking in.

Good fucking deal.

He'd lost precious minutes wrestling his way out of the mostly demolished van, scraping his belly a good one on a chunk of glass from the windscreen in the process, a long, shallow scratch he'd barely noticed in the symphony of misery his body was playing.

When he'd taken in the scale of the destruction, he had to admit that both passengers coming out walking wounded was some kind of twisted miracle. He'd been lucky in another way; the van had landed on the towpath of the canal. This was excellent for two reasons; one, the van could easily have landed *in* the canal, which would have been decidedly unpleasant, and two, fucking Emma had given Keith her address to drive to, and her street overlooked this same canal.

Which meant Keith knew which way Emma had gone.

All he had to do was catch up with her before she got there, then twist her arm for the location of the case. And as long as it was still there…

Keith left that thought unfinished, concentrating on putting one foot in front of the other as quickly as his aching frame would allow. He kept thinking about that limp he'd seen as she'd disappeared into the fog, hoping it had gotten worse, that she'd developed a stitch, or a sprain, or a spontaneous fucking fracture that left her immobile.

I don't have that kind of luck, he thought, teeth gritted against the discomfort he felt each time his feet impacted the rough ground of the towpath, keeping his mind focussed on the suitcase full of crisp twenties.

His for the taking.

All he had to do was keep moving.

Except he'd been moving for ten minutes at least, and the canal was getting close to the girl's street - actually had reached the bottom of it, though Keith knew from the house number she lived halfway up, on the other side of the only bridge crossing for a mile - and no sign of her. It was like she'd been swallowed up by the fucking fog, and what kind of bullshit was this weather, anyway? Never seen anything like it. Supposed to be global *warming,* fucks sake, not this bollocks.

Keith forced himself to walk faster, his left knee protesting the increased pace, what felt like a pretty deep bone bruise adding its voice to the ragged chorus of outrage from his central nervous system.

Well, fuck it all, Keith thought. Fuck the pain. A suitcase full of money would pay for a fuckload of groovy painkillers, and a hot little Thai nurse to feed them to him, before giving him a full-service back massage and a blow job every couple of hours, until he was feeling better enough to fuck her properly...

He felt a stab of self-loathing at that last thought - *getting lustful over a chink, for fuck's sake, disgusting* - but it drained away as he heard a child's voice ahead.

He couldn't make out the words, but it was Emma's voice. She was talking to herself.

Keith grinned.

Keep talking, you stupid little bitch. Go on with your self-soothing bullshit. In a minute I'll give you something to self-soothe about.

He walked faster, ignoring the pain, feeling only vaguely the fresh wave of sweat that slicked his body and face, stepping from his heels to mask his footsteps. A few more agonising seconds and he made out her silhouette, shoulders up against the cold and walking slowly, the sound of her voice resolving into words.

"...she will be cross, but you're right, she'll be so

relieved to see me it'll probably be okay. And there was the bad man. And the car crash. I think I'll start there, tell her I was in a crash…do you think I'll need an ambulance?"

Emma glanced to her right as she spoke, as though she were talking with someone beside her, but she was right on the canal edge, so unless she was talking to a fish…

Fucking kids. Mental, the lot of them, thought Keith, closing the distance as fast as he dared as the girl prattled on.

"Well, it does hurt a bit…Yeah, he looked like he'd fallen out of a tree! Me too, I hope I never see him again…"

Keith knew an entrance line when he heard it. He grabbed her right arm, just below the shoulder, gripping hard enough to really hurt. "Sorry to disappoint…"

"Rachel!" she screamed the name, her pitch and volume drilling into Keith's skull. *Who the fuck is Rachel?* he thought.

Then something solid and very hard collided with his balls, and the thought left his mind as the air whooshed out of his lungs.

He felt his knees starting to give; the explosion of pain rolled up from his nuts across his abdomen, the contents of his stomach suddenly threatening an express evacuation procedure. Emma rotated her arm at the same time, fast, to twist out of his grip. Keith tightened his fist, focussing all his energy on not letting go - *no, you fucking DON'T* - which made him stumble forward, centre of gravity slipping. Emma took a half step away from him, arm moving inside the sleeve of her jacket, and Keith realised he was overextended, was going to fall. *Fuck it,* he thought as he pushed forward with his legs, accelerating the fall, trying to close his fist around the girl's arm. He heard the pitch of her scream twist higher as he pulled her down with him, her arm trapped between them, his weight across her lower body.

The impact of the ground sent pain shooting across Keith's shoulders and down his neck, and he felt the burning heat of scraped skin across his knee. The girl twisted, drawing in breath to shriek again. Ignoring the pain in his shoulders, he brought his fist down on the side of her head with a grunt that was almost a snarl.

The sound her head made as it collided with the rough gravel path was solid, like wood on wood. Keith felt the impact all the way up his arm to his neck; this time the sound he made was a growl of pain.

For a second, Keith felt floaty, disconnected. He blinked rapidly, breath coming in ragged gasps, wiping his sweating face with the sleeve of his jacket.

His vision refocused. There was blood under Emma's head, quite a bit of it, and the eye he could see was already swelling shut from the blow, but she was still breathing, panting fast, her outbreaths tiny whimpers that could almost have been sighs.

Keith got his breathing more under control, shifted his weight, and moved to a kneeling position, legs either side of Emma's torso. He rolled her over, wincing at the pain in his shoulder.

The right side of her face was a mass of purple and red patches; with several small cuts where the gravel had cut into her cheek, her chin. Her nose was also bleeding freely. Her right eye seemed intact, though it was currently screwed shut, tears leaking out from behind it.

Keith leaned right, reaching out with his hand, feeling for the edge of the canal. He found it, lowered his cupped hand into the shockingly cold water, then splashed it over Emma's face.

Her good eye opened immediately, pupil dilating then contracting as she focussed on Keith's face. Her jaw dropped, and Keith clamped the dripping hand over her mouth, leaning in close, kissing distance. She flinched but maintained eye contact, tears still flowing, chest hitching.

Keith held the moment, took a deep breath, and reached for his trademark charming grin.

"Now, Emma, we're going to go and get my fucking money. All right?"

She nodded, good eye wide open, staring so hard it was practically bugging out.

Good fucking deal.

9:45 am

Luke slid the key into his front door lock, then shifted his deployed baton to his right hand.

He'd assumed the worst when he saw the broken windows; shattered glass covering the sofa he, Rob, and Major had spent so many evenings snuggled up on, the magazines from the side table scattered across the carpet, curtain rail torn down. Worst of all, no response when he'd called Rob's name.

There was a bloodstain on one of the ragged chunks of glass left in the window frame. Luke had stared at it for a long second before pulling himself together and heading back to the porch.

Their ageing Zafira was still sat on the driveway, undamaged, and the front door of the house was intact. The perps could have gotten in through the windows, of course, and they could have left the same way, or simply closed the front door behind them…

Or they could still be in there.

Luke's fist tightened on the grip of the baton. He hoped they weren't.

But a deeper part of him hoped they were.

He opened the door fast, one foot on the frame, the other planted behind him, wide stance for balance.

The hallway yawned back at him, looking exactly as he'd left it in the ancient past of yesterday evening, when dinosaurs still roamed the earth, and he was an officer of the law rather than a fugitive from it.

Luke held a slow three count, then crossed the threshold.

"Major?"

The answering bark from upstairs was immediate, and Luke felt a flood of relief. Major wasn't allowed upstairs, but his primary directive was to protect Luke and Rob, and the house, in that order. Which also meant...

"Luke?"

Rob's voice was trembly but clear.

"Here," Luke called, already moving, taking the stairs two at a time, keeping himself under control, keeping the tension in his arm, eyes scanning for signs of ambush, struggle, hope locked down and squirming in his throat...But the landing was clear, the bedroom door was open, and there Rob sat, on the bed, fingers through Major's collar. Major sat to attention, muscles twitching, wanting to run to Luke but holding onto his training. *Good dog,* thought Luke, then he let the hope out, dropping his baton and sprinting the last few steps to his room, dropping to his knees and pulling Rob into his arms, Rob shaking, sobbing, clinging back tight, the warmth of Major between them, his wagging tail thumping gently against the men's legs.

Luke let himself feel the relief - *he's alive, he's okay, it's okay* - then gently ran his hands over Rob's head, down his back, feeling for injuries, a telltale reaction to the firm pressure of his hand. Rob clung tight and sobbed, and Luke concentrated on his breathing, taking in the familiar scent of his husband, shampoo and fabric softener and something deeper that was just *him,* and then Luke was surprised to find he was crying himself, a bone-deep relief that he'd made it back…

What about Syd?

The thought stopped him mid-sob, his gut tightening, twinges in his legs (still aching from the run), skin all at once prickly, unpleasant. A dull ache behind his eyes.

Fuck it. Fuck me.

He let Rob cry it out for another minute, keeping time with his own breaths, then gently pulled back from the embrace. Rob tightened his grip for a second, his standard pre-hug break squeeze that Luke sometimes found adorable and sometimes annoying and sometimes suffocating (and sometimes all three at once); then the two men faced each other. Rob was pale, eyes bloodshot, but he managed a weak smile, which Luke thought was extremely good news.

"Tell me what happened. Slowly. Keep taking deep breaths. We've got all the time in the world."

That last was a quite outrageous lie - inside Luke, it felt like a drill sergeant was just yelling the word *Syd!* over and over again, at teeth-shattering volume - but experience taught him that with Rob, displays of patience were key. He'd clam up at any expression of aggression or anger, but when he felt safe, he could be surprisingly resilient - even, in his small, strange way, brave.

"Two men. Twenties. From the Tower, I think. White. Heights, I don't know, both similar to me, I think. Hoodies up, and with the light out there, I didn't really see faces. Sorry. I'd be shit at your job." Another small smile, sad, but real. Luke kissed him. Held his eyes.

"I couldn't do your job, either. Five minutes in control, I want to gouge my ears out. Manage a whole call centre? Forget it."

It was an exchange they'd had many times, and one that Luke had tired of long ago, but he understood the power of the ritual, so he played it out. Then, "Never mind them. What happened?"

"They smashed the window. Crowbar, looked like. Didn't even see them, I was watching TV…" *curtain drawn, of course,* Luke thought, burying the frustration he felt, all those conversations about the positive effect of sunlight on a depressed mind, "...at first I thought it was an explosion. Then they kept smashing, one of them tore down the curtain, I dunno, maybe the crowbar got caught in the fabric, it all happened so fast..."

"Shh. Slow, Rob. It's okay. It's done. I'm here. Major's here."

"Major!" Rob's face lit up. "Major was fucking amazing! Once the curtain fell, he went for it, the guy with his arm through the window, Major bit it, the guy screamed, pulled back..." Luke's mind flashed to the blood on the broken glass. *Good dog,* he thought, hand dropping to Majors' broad shoulders, rubbing his back as Rob continued, "Then Major just stood there, barking like a demon. Honestly, I knew *I* was safe, but he still scared me!"

Luke nodded. He'd been Major's handler from a puppy to their joint retirement from the K9 unit two years ago, and Luke had witnessed Major in full attack/defend mode many times. It was an awe-inspiring sight.

"And that was it? They left?"

"Yeah. One of them said, I dunno, 'fuck this, plenty of softer targets', I think. They ran off."

Luke nodded again, feeling a surge of anger. Softer targets. Fucking animals. "You came up here?"

"I was scared, and, I dunno, it seemed the best place. Major came with. Didn't tell him to, he just did. Sat right where he is now. Good dog," and Rob was rubbing behind Major's ears. Major's mouth dropped open, tongue lolling, bright brown eyes fixed on Luke.

"Luke, what's happening? Why did the phone stop working? The internet, too, TV news went off about half an hour ago..." *so much for avoiding that shit because of what it does to your anxiety,* Luke thought, frustration surging once more, compounded by the futility of it, a debate they'd had a million times with fuck all to show for it, "...why the fuck are men trying to break in?"

You have to tell him. And then, you have to tell him that you're leaving, and that you're taking Major with you, and that you need him to stay here.

God fucking help me. Where do I even start?

And then, as he took Rob's hand and looked into his eyes, it occurred to him (and he couldn't help but smile) that he knew exactly where to start.

He'd been rehearsing for years, after all.

"Rob, listen. I love you. But..."

FOODTHING#1 (aka LOOKE aka HUNTLEAD

[only when HARNESS], smell StrongAngryReadyfight) making SoftBark at FOODTHING#2 (aka SOFAMAN aka ROBHUNNY smell ScaredSadLove). FOODTHING#2 arms stroking and FOODTHING#2 face leaking and smell SadSad and MAJOR rub head on leg MAJOR GOODDOG and FOODTHING#2 stroke MAJOR head GOODDOG FeelGood GOODDOG EarScritch ahhhhhhhh

More SoftBark with FOODTHING#1 (smell AngryScared) and FOODTHING#2 (smell SadSad scared FaceLeak) hands hold and FOODTHING#1 touch FOODTHING#2 face and FOODTHING#2 stop stroking MAJOR

MAJOR watching and sniffing and hungry and bored and lie down

FOODTHING#1 with FOODTHING#2 up and go to MAJORDEN and MAJOR follow down and round and past SLEEPPLACE/BIGROOM and through FOODROOM and

OUTSIDE!

OUTSIDE (smell DampNext-doorBADCAT been here near ago and is close and BARKDOG in garden down SunSide side and BADMEN NearFar and FireSmoke FarFar and FearSmell all over) Sound BARKDOG and crying and CrashBreak invisible walls and BADMEN LowBarking FarFar. FOODTHING#2 go into OUTSIDEHOUSE (smell

DustFoodbag but NO EAT BADDOG and OldSeatBedMetalDirt and NOISEPUSHER SMALLFURRIES) FOODTHING#2 LeakFace (smell SadSad) and FOODTHING#2 scritch MAJOR ears and make GOODDOG bark and MAJOR HappyHappy sniff and lick hand (taste SaltSadLove) and FOODTHING#1 close OUTSIDEHOUSE and go back to MAJORDEN and FOODTHING#1 in SMALLROOM (no go no chew LEATHER BADDOG)

SOUND

SMELL

HARNESS!!!!!

MAJOR HUNT GOODDOG GOODDOG HARNESS

SIT

WAIT

SIT

HARNESS ON! MAJOR GODDDOG WORK READY want HUNTLEAD say SEEK! MAJOR ready

WALK

WALK outside to SMALLMETALROOM (smell MAJOR and HUNTLEAD and FOODTHING#2 and BADWATER). HUNTLEAD open back of SMALLMETALROOM and UPBOY and MAJOR jump and HUNTLEAD clip collar and HARNESS to

SMALLMETALROOM BACKLEAD and close INVISIBLEWALLDOOR

HUNTLEAD gets in front of SMALLMETALROOM noise starts SMALLMETALROOM moves

MAJOR waits and is GOODDOG and waits for SEEK and HUNT and remembers taste of BADMAN in MAJORDEN and feel of teeth in SOFTMEAT and CopperTaste and BARK and smell of fear

MAJOR waits for METALROOM to stop moving and hopes for GET HIM

GET HIM, MAJOR

GOODDOG

GOODDOG

9:50 am

Billy ran the escape route through their mind over and over: through the plain metal door at the back of the laundrette, past the poky office and foul-smelling toilet, through the fire escape (Billy had already tested it, confirming both that it would open with a push to the central bar and that the sign about the door being alarmed was a lie). Then the alley down to the supermarket car park, and then…

Then, get a car.

Sure, but how? Best bet would be to jump somebody as they got out from parking up, Billy supposed. Though the noise in the laundrette was so loud that they could hear a dull roaring even with the noise-cancelling headphones snug over their ears, prior to the machines starting to run they'd heard regular enough traffic noise. It couldn't all be Mickey's men ferrying cases.

Comes to it, I can take one of them.

Yeah. If they had to. That would mean coming back around to the laundrette side of the little row of shops, which Billy didn't want to risk.

Because by then, it would all be kicking off.

They forced themselves to focus on the job at hand, running the now ragged-looking twenty-pound notes through the counting machine, then using an elastic band to create a 5K bundle to drop into the crate next to them. The surface they were working on faced out front, so Billy relied mainly on their excellent peripheral vision to track activity outside the window.

The fucking fog, though. That was the problem.

They wouldn't get a lot of warning.

Another frustration/worry was not being able to clue Amy in on what was happening. They'd given her the double-tap signal twice - once on their way to the absolutely wretched-smelling WC, once on the way back - and they'd seen her nonchalantly adjust her seating position, checking the straps of her shoulder bag. The double tap was a generic *Be ready/game on* shorthand they'd developed months ago, a small, easily disguised gesture that was certainly helpful, but, Billy felt, rather inadequate to the situation at hand.

Because Billy's *real* crew was coming.

Billy ran the logic one more time - the need to get themselves *and* Amy out without raising Mickey's suspicions, the need to do it *now,* the need to keep Mickey distracted at the tower long enough for Billy and Amy to hit the lockup and disappear - and came out with the same answer.

Enough, then.

Billy tried to relax their mind, recalling the message they'd sent, using the workarounds on the laptop while they sat in the foul-smelling lavatory, describing Mickey's operation and the location (knowing Mickey would have to stay at the laundromat, with the cash). Saying *take him out now, take out the whole gang easy, pocket the cash.* The plan relied on their own crew being as greedy and shortsighted as Mickey (even if better organised) and they did not disappoint. *On way. Be somewhere else,* was the terse reply.

The message was clear - whoever was coming either didn't know who Billy was, or didn't care; regardless, they'd be treated as part of Mickey's gang. Billy knew they couldn't "be somewhere else" until the attack started; on the other edge of that sword, it meant Billy's real crew weren't expecting Billy to be there when the mayhem erupted. So they weren't planning on bringing Billy in just yet. Safety net? Backup to stay in position if it all went south?

Or - nasty thought, this, but inescapable - was Billy going to be "collateral damage?" *No love lost,* thought Billy, without rancour.

Hence, the escape plan, the double tapping, the uncharacteristic tension in their gut as they counted the money, eyes moving like a metronome between the counter, the clock over the front door, and the fog-shrouded view beyond the shop windows. Billy watched Mickey out there, pacing, occasionally yelling at one of the crew who appeared out of the fog with another case - Billy couldn't hear it over the roar of the machines, but they could see the back of Mickey's bald head flush, read the tightening of his shoulders, clock the reactions of the other men picking up their pace, faces flushed with anger and embarrassment.

Billy's cash counter clicked empty. They rubber banded the bundle, tossed it into the crate, rough stacked the next pile of bills, started the counter, checked the clock - 9:53, too early to expect any action - looked back at the window…

It was, they'd reflect later, exactly like something out of a horror movie.

The figures emerged from the fog like they'd been birthed from it. Black clothes from head to toe - balaclavas, eyes cut wide for better fields of vision, zip-up jumpers, gloves, combat boots. Billy counted twelve, all armed; baseball bats, a couple of knives, one machete…

And one gun.

Billy was already moving, backing towards Amy, not turning to run, turning would be a mistake, running would draw attention, acutely aware how visible they were lit up behind the glass and out of the fog, Mickey moving, Mickey turning and running *fast,* that scary pace of his, face showing something Billy had never seen before; he was fast but not fast enough, Billy could see that, saw the barrel of the pistol lazily rising to attention, like it had all the time in the world, Billy still moving backwards, relying on the map in their head to navigate, feeling Amy's leg against their back, a double tap on her shin, her moving immediately, sliding off her perch, standing behind them, Billy reaching back with their hand, Mickey's slamming open the door, taking a step through, the gun going off, the roar of the spinning money and tumbling gravel turning the gunshot into flash and smoke, like a silent movie, Mickey staggering forwards, face turning from pink to grey, another flash, the plate glass window exploding, the sound just on the edge of hearing, Mickey locking eyes with Billy, mouth moving, no sound but Billy could lip read...

Get her out.

And then Billy turned, not wanting to see more, pulling Amy in front of them, but she saw something, Billy saw her see it, in her face, her eyes, but she moved, fast, fluid, Billy putting their back between her and bullets, pointing, then running to the corridor, pushing her in front, Amy picking up pace with every step...

Billy had time to think *we're going to be okay, as soon as we're through the door we're lost in the fog,* and at that exact moment the fire door ahead swung open. Billy saw the balaclavaed figure, sledgehammer cocking back to swing, Billy still accelerating, Amy in front.

Nowhere to go.

Amy saw the man, the hammer, and the vision of the side of Mickey's face disintegrating in a cloud of red and white was suddenly, blessedly gone.

She had time to think *can't slow down*.

So I'd better speed up.

She did, feeling Billy drop back, the imprint of their body against her back gone. She pushed forward, one step, two, already seeing her acceleration would carry her under the arc of the sledgehammer swing, third step and *slide…*

She dropped on her arse, swinging her feet up, toes of her boots pointed forward. She felt a jolt that ran from ankle to hip as both legs slammed into the figure, twisting her sideways. Something collided with her shoulder as the man pivoted onto his other foot, then the rest of her slammed into his legs and she felt him falling forwards. She tucked in and rolled, like a kid down a hill, one spin, two, three, the blast of cold, damp air telling her she'd made it out.

She heard a crunch from behind her, Billy grunting in pain. She scrambled to her feet and turned, body thrilling with adrenaline.

The man she'd hit was lying on his side, top half propped up by the corridor wall, struggling to stand. The head of the sledgehammer was embedded in the opposite wall, swallowed by a gaping hole in the plasterboard.

So was Billy's left hand.

Billy placed their free palm against the wall, pulling the trapped hand free with a growl of pain. Amy caught a glimpse of red, purple and white, covered in a shower of plaster dust, before returning her attention to the man in the balaclava.

He'd got a knee under him and was starting to rise to his feet, reaching for the sledgehammer.

Amy took a step forward and swung her right arm, fingers folded and thumb tucked alongside as she'd practised, hitting the man's temple with the heel of her palm as hard as she could. The man's head collided with the wall, the shockwave of the blow jarring Amy's shoulder. Her peripheral vision caught the man's hands releasing the handle of the hammer.

Movement from behind him caused her to look up in time to see Billy's foot swinging towards the man's chin.

Amy jumped back as Billy's foot collided with the man's face. Amy saw the man's jaw go sideways under the balaclava, and a splash of spit and blood sprayed out as he fell backwards. He hit the deck, hands moving to his face, a mushy moan coming from his suddenly slightly off-kilter jaw line. Billy used their good hand to pull the sledgehammer from the wall. The head came loose in a shower of white dust that covered the writhing, moaning man. Billy looked down at him, and Amy read the calculation on her lover's face. Apparently coming to the same conclusion she had - the man was no longer a threat, and the roaring of the machines in the laundrette would cover the sound of his cries - Billy stepped over him and joined Amy in the alley. Amy saw they were sweating, pale; their ruined hand hung limply by their side.

Their eyes met.

Mickey's dead.

The thought held no weight, yet she could feel it in her mind, an impossibly huge object, threatening to eclipse her mind, plunge everything else into darkness. A moment she'd dreamed about since she was seven years old, imagined a million times, a thousand scenarios…

And now it had come, she was relieved and ashamed to discover there was no time to mark it, no time at all; they had to run, *now,* get a ride, get to the lockup, somehow pick the lock with Billy's good hand smashed to a pulp…

Life goes on.

Amy nodded. Billy nodded back. They held out the sledgehammer. Amy took it, holding the handle up near the head, then held out her other hand.

Billy took it.

Leaving the roaring machines and damaged man behind them, they ran into the fog.

9:55 am

Keith stopped walking, keeping both grips firm - one on the handle of the black suitcase, filled with more cash than Keith had ever seen in his life, the other around the back of Emma's neck.

The pain was worse. His shoulders and neck kept sending random stabs as he walked, there was some kind of headache brewing, and his balls felt swollen from the swift kick Emma had somehow managed to land on him earlier. Still, he was feeling happy. The money was *real,* it was *his,* and best of all, nobody but him even knew it existed.

Well. Okay. One other.

But not for long.

"What did you say?" He was grinning as he spoke, though looking at her ruined face, he wasn't sure Emma could even see him. Her right eye had swollen shut completely, and the eyelid on the left was fluttering, caked with blood from the gash on her forehead. She was somehow putting one foot in front of the other as he dragged her along, staggering forward; autopilot or just momentum, Keith supposed. Taking in her ruined face, one of his favourite jokes swam into his mind -

what do you tell a woman with two black eyes? Nothing, you've already told her twice - and he chuckled.

"Et. Eee oh"

Her jaw was barely moving, lips a swollen bloody pulp, blood running freely from her nose - Keith remembered the pain of her teeth biting into his knuckles as he punched her face - *take that, mouthy bitch* - still, the words popped into his mind, *let me go.* He replied in the cheery tone he used in the pub when regaling the lads with some story or other about his latest exploits with the missus, "Of course I will! Any minute now!"

"Eeese. Eeese," She was fading now, voice getting bubbly, footsteps faltering, but that was okay, they'd come far enough. He took one final step towards the edge of the canal, and with a cheery, "Here you go," shoved her forward, one hand on her neck, the other in the small of her back. His shoulders and back protested loudly at the exertion as her body toppled forward, hitting the canal water face down and immediately slipping under the surface.

Keith watched, feeling a coldness run through him, as though, just for a second, he was experiencing what she must be, in her last moments; the icy embrace of the water squeezing the breath and heat out of her.

She resurfaced as her body's natural buoyancy brought her up. There was no current acting on her, but the momentum from the push meant she slowly drifted into the centre of the canal. As Keith watched she rolled onto her back, arms and legs flailing in what looked to him like the spastic motions of a landed fish. She vomited a stream of blood and grimy water, then emitted a single, shuddering sob.

For just a moment, an image of Patsy came into his mind, fallen from the swing, skinned knee, running to him, hugging him tight and fierce, hugging the pain out, her tears on his shirt, him being *Dad,* wondering at the simple magic of the moment, and he felt something lurch in his chest. He tightened his grip on the handle of the case until his arm muscles ached and pushed the image out of his mind, replacing it with the contents of the case, the reality of *that;* the new life it gave him, free of Patsy and Jenine and ToyZ N GamZ and the wankers down the pub and all that shit.

By the time the weight of her wet clothes dragged Emma's head back under for the last time, Keith's mind was already turning away from what he'd done, engaging instead with the pressing urgency of what to do next.

How to make a clean getaway.

Rachel floats in the water as her best friend drowns.

She floats face to face with Emma, bodies turning in parallel. Rachel sees the last of Emma leave her, a slow stream of bubbles escaping from her suddenly waxen lips. As the bubbles pass through her, Rachel catches the very last of Emma's thoughts.

Rachel, stop him, please, make him stop, I'm sorry Mum, I'm sorry Santa, I love you, I'm sorry…

Emma's body sinks to the bottom of the canal and lays there, face up. Rachel floats above her, looking down.

Seconds pass. Rachel is still here.

Emma is gone.

It's wrong. Rachel knows that. She's a creature of imagination, made real only by Emma's mind, need, loneliness. Sure, sometimes brighter than Emma (the art is often wiser than the artist) but nonetheless…

As if the thought has caused the world to notice this aberration, Rachel begins to feel a coldness creeping into her. Rachel has never experienced physical sensations, beyond the impact of Emma's high fives and the occasional hug (because, Rachel realises, those were the only things Emma needed/wanted her to feel) but now…

What can I do? Rachel askes Emma, but Emma is beyond replying. Rachel feels the cold spreading within her, numbing, and Rachel supposes she's dying, the way Emma has died, and maybe what's left of Rachel is, like the residual body heat of Emma, being leeched away by the cold water…

Rachel, stop him, please make him stop, I'm sorry Mum, I'm sorry Santa, I love you, I'm sorry…

The words come back to Rachel. Emma's final commandment. But Rachel is nothing without Emma's spark, her vivid imagination. *I can't do anything,* she thinks, staring at the thing that was Emma, already settling into the mud of the canal bed.

Sure, you can.

The thought comes from Rachel, not Emma, but of course it's Emma's injunction to herself, spoken through Rachel, and, *okay, I'm imaginary, cool,* thinks Rachel, *that means I can do anything.*

So.

Make him stop.

And then Rachel thinks *fly,* and suddenly Rachel is hovering above the canal and she can see them all, as she casts her gaze to the row of houses behind the fog. She can see the fog and the houses in the fog and the people in the houses and the dull grey thread of their pasts and the many multicoloured threads of their possible futures, each strand collapsing into their centres as the seconds pass and the multitude of possibilities die out, decision by decision, breath by breath, and she hears the singing of the strands, hears the destinations each strand represents, the ones that lead to many more branches of possibility ringing like an orchestral crescendo, the ones that lead to thinner branches emitting a smaller, sadder tone…

And she knows what she must do.

She finds him shambling away from the bank of the canal, dragging the case behind him. Sees the strands flowing from his stomach, the grey dead past tangling with the end of Emma's strands (Emma's already faint as well as grey, returning to the fog, and Rachel feels the coldness spreading out from her own centre, numbing, unravelling, becoming less - how long before Emma's strands are gone? How long before Rachel is gone with them?). A handful of strands flow from Keith's centre. Most of them are singing with a lustrous tone, but Rachel sees one that plays a single blue note, the thread itself pale, almost grey, and she touches the thread. Instantly the cold insider her intensifies, but she sees…

She can't tell if it's an ending, but the thread collapses into a tangle with many others, very near, very soon. The noise of the tangle is discordant and loud and she can't differentiate it, but she sees the greyness of *this* particular strand, and thinks of Emma, and realises it's the only chance she's got.

Rachel touches the thread, goes *inside* the thread (*sure, you can*), following the thread up from his stomach into his mind. It's full of hammers and shadows and blood and women's screams. She concentrates on the thread, finds it connecting with thoughts of *buying a car from Dodgy Del and driving to London and finding an old connection that can make him a fake passport*. She sees the idea floating among a series of others, some vivid and powerful, some half-formed and grey, and Rachel *pushes* and the cold spreads, deepening, terrifying, but Rachel sees the other threads fall away, leaving only the pale grey strand, and as Keith opens the case and takes two bundles of money to place in his jacket pocket, then closes it up and follows that faint thread, Rachel follows, sharp cold eating its way through what's left of her, holding on as hard as she can, to herself, to her memory of Emma…

To hope.

Hour 3

10:00 am -

10:00 am

MAJOR SEEK.

SEEK two scents. ONE FEMALEHUMANPUP (smell StrongPurpleFearSweatBLOODFakeorangefruitSoap). OTHER is MAN (smell SmokeSweatAngerFearBLOODBadDrink). MAJOR hopes OTHERMAN is BADMAN. Hopes GET HIM, MAJOR

(other smells: WaterMudOtherDOGS, BADCATS, MEN FEMALE SQUIRELL BIRBS but MAJOR has HARNESS, is WORK, is GOODDOG and does not SNIFF or CHASE gooddog gooddog)

Stones and mud under paws. Moving FastWalk, FOODTHING#1 moving FastWalk. Can't see far (GreyWall) but scents clear, MAJOR happy, MAJOR SEEK

MAJOR FIND BIGSMALLMETALROOM and smells FEMALEHUMANPUP and BadWater OTHERMANBLOOD (all scents inside, FruitSoapSmokeBLOODFear) BIGSMALLMETALROOM and POINT

POINT

FOODTHING#1 moves to

BIGSMALLMETALROOM and looks and looks and MAJOR

POINT

WAIT

POINT

FOODTHING#1 brings InvisibleWallPiece with BLOOD and SEEK, MAJOR

POINT

FOODTHING#1 POINT AWAY from BIGSMALLMETALROOM, brings BLOOD to MAJOR face, SEEK, MAJOR

MAJOR SEEK and back away from BIGSMALLMETALROOM. Faster. Scents stronger. FOODTHING#1 faster and run and SEEK and OTHERBLOOD smell stronger and FEMALEHUMANPUP stronger then MuchBlood and FEMALEHUMANPUP scent go to water and stop but OTHERMANBLOODSmokeAnger strong and MAJOR, SEEK and MAJOR SEEK and RUN, hoping for BADMAN and GET HIM, MAJOR

SEEK

10:05 am

"This…is yours?"

Amy loved the note of admiration in Billy's voice, which she could hear even through the strain. Her lover was clearly in a lot of pain, their wounded hand held protectively against their chest, breathing ragged from the short run, sweat running down their pale face. Still, Billy was grinning at her, and the weight across her chest and shoulders lightened for a moment.

She looked back at the car. It was, she had to admit, a class act. An ugly, shit-brown Toyota, fifteen years old. It was such a sorry sight that nobody had bothered to vandalise it, even though it had sat, apparently mouldering, in the street outside the tower for months. As she'd hoped, it had become part of the scenery almost immediately.

She put her hand into her right jacket pocket, through the hole she'd made in the lining of her coat, found the car fob, and released the locks. "Your carriage awaits," she said, smiling and sketching a curtsey. Billy grunted a laugh, then opened the passenger side door, carefully avoiding using their damaged hand. Amy saw this; remembered the bleeding, pulped flesh she'd glimpsed under the makeshift bandage she'd fashioned from her vest, Billy's gritted teeth and low moan of pain as she'd tightened it up.

Behind that image, another floated up; the man with his sledgehammer raised; then Mickey, looking not at her but at Billy, just before the side of his face disintegrated, his right eye and half his forehead turning to a red and white cloud. She'd already been turning away, had only glimpsed it, but it was seared into her memory, raw, burning, furious.

"Amy, love?" Amy blinked fast a couple of times, opened the rear passenger door, slung the sledgehammer across the back seat then opened the driver's side door and climbed in.

"How are you holding up?" She had to laugh. There they were, hand smashed to shit by a lunatic with a sledgehammer, no painkillers, still asking after her. But Billy missed nothing, she knew that; it was a big part of why she loved them, their attentiveness. And Amy could always be herself with them, always just tell the truth. That had a value beyond reckoning.

"Freaked, Billy. Can't get the image of Mickey dying out of my head. He was a shitbag, and he deserved it, and I know it's something we talked about, but…" she trailed off, tears in her eyes. Billy's good hand found hers.

"Yeah. I get it."

And Amy knew they did.

"Painkillers're in the glovebox," she said, changing the subject. Billy opened it up, retrieved the box of co-codamol, stared at it for a second, then handed it to Amy with an apologetic shrug. "Guess I'll be playing nurse for a while", she said primly (which made Billy smile, a real one, like the sun coming out from behind a cloud), then opened the box, removing two tablets from the blister pack and handing them to Billy. They dry swallowed the tablets, then turned to Amy.

"So, where did you get this?" Amy was surprised by the question - and a little concerned, it wasn't like Billy not to think it through - then relieved as they joined in with her answer, "Dodgy Del's," both smiling. It felt good, in spite of everything - this wasn't how they'd planned it, but they had a clear out; likely wouldn't be missed for days or even weeks, with all the lunacy going on, and Mickey...

Oh, but that hurt to think about.

She'd hated him; hated him to her bones. The way he'd controlled her, decided who she could and couldn't sleep with, not by punishing her, but by punishing *them*. She'd fantasised about killing him. She was glad he was gone. She wouldn't mourn him.

But, she was discovering, she'd *really* rather not have seen it.

"Are you set to drive?" The question pulled her back

to the moment.

"Yes, I think so. Wish I'd spent more time practising picking that lock, though."

Billy held up their bandaged hand, then gestured at the back seat, "Sure, but on the other hand…"

Yes, she thought, she could probably smash the entire lock off with that, now stealth was no longer an issue. "Fair enough." She tightened her grip on the steering wheel, knuckles whitening, trying to *see* it, the way she had so many times, so many different ways; her and Billy, the lockup, the car loaded with crates of Mickey's cash, off into the happy ever after, trying to make it real.

She couldn't do it.

Billy's good hand covered hers, gently caressing as they spoke. "Take your time, lover. We've got this. *You've* got this. Nobody knows the money's there, nobody's going looking for it, and we're never going to have better cover to evaporate than today's insanity. We're home free. Okay?"

Amy nodded, wanting it to be true so badly it hurt.

Billy squeezed her hand. "I know, love. But trust me. Trust *us*."

Amy found, to her relief, that she did. She took a long, deep breath, then, on the exhale, started the car. The engine turned over smoothly. The tower block loomed behind her, a grey pillar of concrete wreathed in fog, the top half concealed such that, looking up, one might suppose it rose forever. She saw it in the rearview mirror without really seeing it at all, a landmark of her young life as familiar as the back of her own hand. She put the car in gear and pulled away, and by the time she looked back, it was gone, swallowed by the fog.

Neither of them would ever see it again.

10:10 am

Rachel is fading fast, now, the coldness becoming numbness as parts of her lift off and float away, joining with the fog that surrounds her, them, everyone. She longs to drift apart completely, become Nothing and All and One. The lights of the threads shine through the mist; she knows from high enough she could see it all, laid out like a map of the neural pathways of the mind of the world, the people just a few billion firing synapses bouncing into and off of each other, the beautiful chaos creating an impossible impressionistic tapestry; the vomit splatter of a mad god…

Rachel stop him.

She pulls herself back to Keith, as he walks along the grey strand, the light in the thread dimming, the note it chimes with singular and blue, but then suddenly there's a new split, close up ahead. In one direction the thread thins further, becoming almost translucent, but the other branch glows vibrantly, and looking further along it, Rachel can see a spouting of vivid bright pathways, like the tendrils of a sea anemone.

This will not do.

Rachel pulls back to see where the dim thread leads - she has to see, but it's risky; the fog is pulling at her, plucking her apart, strand by strand - and she sees it pass through an open gate into an L-shaped space, the gate at the tip of the short edge, the long containing a row of garages on both sides. Two men are getting out of a large white van with a dent in the rear left hand side. She drifts closer and from their threads she hears that they are both Bobby and are here to TAKE...

And Keith's grey thread tangles with them and others she doesn't know, there's blood and pain and threads ending...she can't see for sure if Keith's thread ends, it's too tangled, but there's no time because Keith is approaching the branch and she has to move him NOW. She touches the thread and she's back in his mind as he approaches the gate, and the split, and he's thinking

(*a motor from Del that's the ticket London Jim'll hook me up with papers fucker owes me from hey lockup's open someone must be oh well got the case no need for greed just*)

She sees he's about to turn away, so she focusses with what little is left of her will and sends him the word

TAKE

and she sees his thoughts shift

(*no need to get greedy just stash the case take a quick shufti might be something tasty, nobody's about don't look a gift horse in the mouth, Keith, Dad always said*)

She sees Keith has passed the branching moment, is back on the dim, thin thread, stalking over to a nearby hedgerow and pushing the case into it, and she floats up, feeling lighter than air, lighter than thought, seeing the bloody tangle he is now heading into and hoping…

MAJOR SEEK OTHERMANBLOOD smell stronger, FEMALEHUMANPUP (FakefruitSoapScent) there but old, NotFresh, RubOff, FEMALEHUMANPUP scent not there but smell of her on OTHERMAN [BADMAN?] and OTHERMAN getting close) and MAJOR not PULL, MAJOR is GoodDog, MAJOR SlowFastWalk and FOODTHING#1 SLowFastWalk (smell some like FEMALEHUMANPUP and FEMALEHUMANPUP came from FOODTHING#1). Is GOOD.

MAJOR SEE

OTHER(BADMAN?) scent very close, goes two ways, MAJOR smells way through opening in Wall (and another BIGSMALLMETALROOM and BadWater and other MEN and SmokeSweat) and MAJOR smells other scent of OTHER(BADMAN?) and MAJOR follows that scent and

SEEKS and finds BLACKBOX in VerySmallTree and

POINT

POINT

Billy's nodding off, thanks to the codeine/adrenaline comedown combo, so it's Amy alone who sees the problem. The gate to the lockup is open.

She pulls over, trying to slow down her heart rate, trying to *think*.

Plenty of people have the gate combo. Any of the people who rent one of the other units could...

But she's kept the car creeping forward as she's pulled up to the kerb, and that's not what's going on; the ancient push button lock (*X52Y*, she thinks, reflexively) is smashed to hell and the handle below it is dangling off and the gate's pushed open wide enough to admit a vehicle. The fog conceals what's going on inside, but...

Well, shit, she thinks.

She doesn't want to wake Billy, so she does it as gently as possible, shaking the shoulder above their undamaged hand. They come to instantly, but she notices the way their pupils dilate and eyes roll for just a second before focussing on her face.

She points at the gate. Billy takes it in.

"Well, shit."

"Yeah," she says, already coming to a decision. She undoes her seatbelt and turns to Billy, meeting their eyes. "I'm going to go take a look. Strictly recon. You watch the road. Honk if anyone shows. Keep your door open. If I yell out…"

"Got it." Billy is already reaching over to the backseat, grabbing the sledgehammer with their good hand, offering it to Amy with a raised eyebrow.

"No. It'll only slow me down. You bring it if you need it."

"Cavalry on standby."

"Good. I won't need it," she says, but she's not sure that's true. The fucking fog is the problem; as soon as she's through the gate, she's invisible to Billy, but drive any closer and the car engine might alert whoever's in there (*if it hasn't already,* a treacherous voice that sounds suspiciously like that of her dead brother tells her).

On the other hand, if she's careful, they won't see her coming.

She realises she's certain someone is there.

Well, shit, she thinks, one more time. Then she turns to Billy, kisses them on the cheek, and opens the door, stepping out and closing it as softly as she can.

She takes one last look at the pale but alert face of her lover through the windscreen.

Then, moving quickly and quietly, she crosses the distance to the open gate and walks through, crouching low.

FOODTHING#1 brings BLACK BOX and MAJOR smells OTHER(BADMAN) and FEMALEHUMANPUP and FEMALEHUMANPUP blood and MAJOR has FOUND and MAJOR is GOODDOG and FOODTHING#1 touched FEMALEHUMANPUPBLOOD and OTHER(BADMAN?) blood and tells MAJOR GOODDOG YES AM GOODDOG GOODDOG and tells MAJOR SEEK

and

Rachel sees the young woman going through the gate, behind Keith by no more than a couple of minutes, but he's crouched down in the corner, catching his breath and listening carefully, and Rachel sees him see her walk past, and she sees the other threads in the tangle brighten and then there's a policeman and his dog at the gate, and the person in the car across the street (whose thread is tangled with the young woman's, wrapped around each other like a plait) is sat up and reaching behind them for a hammer and the young woman is

moving at a low crouch past the chain link fence to the right that separates the lockup from a vacant office, heading left, to the brick wall of the first of the units. Amy moves quickly, eyes fixed ahead, on the point where she knows the corner of the building is, willing it to emerge from the fog. As it does, her ears tune in to bad news; feet crunching across the loose gravel, at least two pairs, grunting, swearing, low male voices; she can't make out the words but there's a horrible familiarity to the tone. She slows down, placing each step carefully, moving as close to silently as she can, the corner of the building edging closer. *Mickey's lockup is three doors down.*

You'll be able to see them, but they'll be able to see you. Keep low. Stay smart. Report back.

And as she draws closer, the voices become clearer, and that sinking feeling in her stomach intensifies, because of course it's the two fucking Bobbies and their fucking van, of course they knew where Mickey's lockup was, and of course they somehow survived the carnage at the laundrette, and of course they're going to take the money and fucking run (or even take it and stay, the fucking idiots) , and Amy thinks *gotta get back to Billy,* because, yes, two on two, pound for pound, they can drop the Bobbies easy enough (*as long as they're not armed,* sure, okay, thank you for that)

Rachel sees Keith start moving, low and fast, grimacing and sweating, closing with the young woman with her back to him, Rachel sees the tangle and the blood but it's too late now, and anyway

(*Rachel, stop him*)

it was the only way, so she watches and hopes and

the sound of gravel crunching underfoot reaches Amy at the same time as a flicker in her peripheral vision and the smell of sweat and blood. She turns fast, and sees a nightmare shambling toward her; huge bags under bloodshot eyes, a face pale and sweaty with hectic redness in the cheeks, blood caking his nose and grimacing mouth, a security guard uniform; damp, dark splashes in the black material, arm pulling back, fist raised and

MAJOR sits at opening in Wall and scent of BLOOD goes through (scent of OTHER hope is BADMAN HopeHopeHope GET HIM MAJOR) and FOODTHING#1 says WAIT. FOODTHING#1 gets out HITTING STICK for BADMEN.

MAJOR WAIT.

WAIT.

GOODDOG.

WAIT.

Rachel, floating higher now, sees the young woman start to duck as Keith swings a fist towards her head, and the blow connects with the wall behind her as the person in the car steps out, sledgehammer in hand, behind the policeman and dog who do not see or hear, focussed ahead, the dog's nose twitching at Keith's greying thread, muscles bunched under dark fur, and

Amy is running, and she hears her attacker bellow with pain, feet on gravel, he's coming after her, and behind that the Bobbies also cry out, moving her way, and Amy is still accelerating, drawing breath to scream her lover's name, as the gate comes into view as she sees

FRESHEXCITEDSCAREDFEMALE running and MAJOR WAIT and OTHER is coming and BIGSMALLMETALROOM is making NOISE and MAJOR WAITS and WAITS and IS READY and FRESHEXCITEDSCAREDFEMALE

the young woman yells at the policeman "he's after me," and the fear is real and the pain is real but it's also an act and Rachel sees the person with the hammer crouch by his open car door as precious seconds tick by and the woman runs towards the policeman and

Amy sees the policeman nod and gesture to his right, so she changes the angle of her run, aiming to hit the gap between the policeman and his dog and the gate, and she has time to see the cop notice her change of direction and yell

"GET BADMAN, MAJOR"

MAJOR running and BADMAN is ScaredAngryHurt and slows but MAJOR is fast and GOODDOG and MAJOR jumps and jaws close and pierce and rip and grip and BADMAN makes NoisePain and is DELICIOUS and

Rachel is slipping away, zooming out, too soon, too late, and one of the Bobbies sees Keith on the ground and the dog biting, gripping, ripping, and starts to run forward but then sees the policeman closing in and yells and turns and the

van starts to accelerate and

Amy, skidding to a halt and turning, sees it all.

She sees the man who tried to attack her squirming on the floor, shrieking in pain and fear, the dog on top of him a mess of fur and muscle and teeth snarling deep and low, spraying him with saliva and his own blood.

She sees the man grab the dog's front legs and pull them in opposite directions. The howl of pain from the dog cuts through the man's screams, and the revving of the engine behind him. The dog twists free of the man's grip and falls onto the concrete, chest heaving, whimpering. The policeman changes direction, dropping his baton and sliding to his knees beside the fallen dog. She can't see his face, but the slump of his shoulders tell their own story.

And then, the headlights.

The van is coming fast, straight at the policeman and the dog.

And after that, her.

Move, thinks Amy, and she does, but it's like she's moving through treacle, suddenly, a nightmare where the air is too thick and everything she's trying to do is too slow, too late. As she turns, the last thing she sees is the policeman throwing the dog out of the path of the van, the van swerving, and she sees it'll miss the dog but it'll clearly hit the cop, and the man who attacked her who is still struggling to his feet, then she's facing the gate and running as hard as she's ever run, slamming each leg down, willing for forward momentum, acceleration, and she hears two damp thumps followed by snapping sounds and still the van engine revs higher, louder and she's through the gate and starting to pivot to the left when the impact takes her on her side and knocks her off her feet.

MAJOR   HURT   FOODTHING#1HURT BIGSLEEP HURT MAJOR PAIN BADMAN BIGSLEEP MAJOR HURT HURT HURT MAJOR GOODDOG
GOODDOG
FOODTHING#1 BIGSLEEP
GOODDOG
HURT
(smell FRESHEXCITEDSCAREDFEMALEHurt)

Rachel's vision is fading, her self spreading into the fog (or the fog into her), but she sees the van still accelerating, veering drunkenly across the street before mounting the pavement and colliding head-on into the brick wall of Dodgy Del's garage. The two men inside crash through the windscreen, heads colliding with the wall, the cracking of their skulls sounding like twin pistol shots.

Rachel draws her focus away from their ragdoll remains and drifts toward Keith. She sees his thread has faded almost to nothing, will soon end entirely, and what's left is vibrating with elemental pain. It should be savagely satisfying, but what's left of Rachel can only experience a vague, tired sense of relief.

As she drifts more, she sees the policeman is already gone, and the dog (hurt, but Rachel sees his thread, vibrant and branching; he'll live) has crawled over to his master, is licking the blood and tears from his sightless eyes, and beyond that, she sees

Amy opens her eyes.

Billy smiles down at her. "Cavalry reporting for duty, ma'am."

She grins back. In a second, she knows the adrenaline will wear off, and she'll feel the pain from the side of her body that hit the pavement after Billy rugby tackled her out of the path of the van. But as far as she's concerned, that's a problem for the future.

Right now, she's alive and in the arms of her lover, and life tastes very sweet indeed.

Now is forever, she thinks, and kisses Billy.

10:15 am

What's left of Rachel feels the lovers come closer to the howling dog and the broken body of the policeman. The woman reaches out and touches the dog's fur, and it's a beautiful thing to fade out on, but Rachel sees the pain in the dog and the longing in the woman, and with the very last of her will, she winds the two threads together, and as the effort causes the last of her to dissipate, the woman says

"Dylan!" Amy would never know what made the name pop into her mind at that precise moment, but as soon as she said it, it felt, right, obvious, and the Alsatian looked up at her, its sad brown eyes meeting her own and

Millionaires Day

DILLON am DILLON MAJOR is DILLON and is
GOODDOG and WAG and FRESHFEMALE is
FOODTHING#1 and DILLON is GOODDOG
GOODDOG

10:30 am

It took Amy and Billy fifteen minutes to fill their car with crates of Mickey's cash, and by the time they'd done so, the fog had mostly lifted. Even with the boot, the passenger footwell, and half the backseat full to capacity, there were still half a dozen crates left in the van. Amy thought there were likely more in the lockup, but when Billy said that what they had would be enough, she agreed wholeheartedly. She did take one final crate over to the passenger side door and stuffed as many bundles of cash as she could into the glove box, before leaving the crate open on the pavement (where it would be found, half an hour after they drove away, by a homeless man named Henry Jones, who would look into the crate, at the bodies from the van and the lockup driveway, shake his head, then fill his pockets with a few bundles of cash before walking away, head lowered, muttering to himself).

By the time they were ready to roll Billy was exhausted. Amy thought there was a good chance they'd have nodded off before the car hit city limits. She looked in the rearview mirror, straight into the eyes of the Alsatian that sat up on the back seat, ears cocked, mouth slightly open, tongue hanging out.

She smiled at Dylan, said, "Good dog" and enjoyed the sound of his tail whickering against the plastic crates. Then she lowered the rear right window, put the car into gear, and drove herself, her lover and her dog the fuck out of Milton Keynes, never to return.

And as she pulled away from the kerb

DILLON feel breeze MANY SCENTS and head outside SMALLMETALBOX and SUN and BREEZE and MANYSCENTS and LIFE and WAG

DILLON GOODDOG

GOODDOG

Note From the Publisher

Thank you for reading *Millionaires Day*. Whether you liked it or not we hope you'll take a moment to leave a review on Amazon or your favorite book review site. Reviews are vitally important to all of the authors and editors involved, both to help with marketing the book and improving their work in the future. Thank you!

Acknowledgements

First, thanks to Chris Gonzo, the guitarist in my previous band (The Disciples of Gonzo, gone from the charts but not from our hearts) who, on a smoke break from another hectic rehearsal, asked the innocent question ("Why don't they just give everyone a million pounds each?") that led to the story you've just read.

Next, thanks to Kiddo, my now teenage daughter, who helped me unsnarl various plot cul-de-sacs that beckoned at points, and especially for helping me map out the sequencing of the final collision of threads. Appreciate it, kid. Now get back to work on your own novel; it isn't going to write itself.

Thanks to my faithful beta readers Dave Watkins and C.C. Adams: your input made this novella better. Next round's definitely on me.

This novella would likely not have been written at all, and certainly not in the form you've found it, without the music of The Prodigy, specifically their *Invaders Must Die* album - if you're looking for a soundtrack as you read along, you could do a lot worse.

Thanks to Stephen Kozeniewski (one day I'll be

able to type that right first time) for taking a flyer on a Limey author for his US press - hope you're happy with the results. And thanks also to his assistant, author and my first (and so far, only) superfan, Kayleigh Dobbs - your belief in what I do has pushed me to be a better writer. Thank you.

Thanks as always to Jim Mcleod of Gingernuts Of Horror for all your support over the last... shit, **decade**, man, we're getting *old*.

The passing of my old man doesn't seem to have done much, if anything, to reduce the enormously positive impact he has on my life, so; thanks, Dad, and sorry as hell you didn't get to read this one. I think you'd have gotten a kick out of it (especially when you got to the 'money laundering' gag which you gave me when we were talking about the premise, some years back).

And finally, as ever, thanks to my wise, brilliant, and long-suffering wife, for giving me the space and time and support to continue to throw words at the screen. I love you to the moon and back.

About the Author

Kit Power lives in Milton Keynes and mainly writes horror and dark crime fiction, with occasional forays into dystopian science fiction, and nonfiction essays and reviews on pop culture (with a focus on horror and rock music). Described by Happy Goat Horror reviews as "the best horror writer you've never heard of," his novella *A Song For The End* was a finalist for a British Fantasy Society award in 2021, and his essay collection/autobiography, *My Life In Horror Volume II* (based on the long-running Ginger Nuts of Horror series of the same name) was a finalist in the 2022 non-fiction category. He's also an enthusiastic podcaster, with shows covering Sherlock Holmes, James Bond movies, Bruce Springsteen (the latter two also featuring his dear friend James Slater Murphy), writing, short horror stories (*The Ultimate Horror Anthology*, with fellow horror author Jasper Bark), and what he insists on calling "the greatest movie ever made," *RoboCop*. For more about his work, see www.patreon.com/kitpower

Also Available from

French Press Publishing

SPLATTERPUNK AWARD NOMINATED AUTHOR

SOMER CANON

YOU'RE MINE

"TWISTY, DANGEROUS, SEXY, AND TENSE..."
-JONATHAN JANZ, AUTHOR OF THE SIREN AND THE SPECTER AND MARLA

Insecure misfit Ioni Davis never thinks she'll find love in her sleepy West Virginia hometown. Then the tall, fascinating stranger Raber Belliveau transfers to her school.

Their attraction is instant and red-hot. And a shared fascination with witchcraft bonds the young lovers even closer.

But while Ioni is responsibly studying her newfound religion of Wicca, Raber has chosen an altogether…different path.

Soon, Raber's behavior becomes manipulative. Even abusive. And their love story for the ages is turning into a macabre farce. All Ioni wants to do is get out.

But Raber has discovered a dreadful way to control their relationship. A ritual which hasn't been attempted in over a century. A spell to unleash a bloodthirsty terror which can never be satisfied.

Ioni finds herself trapped in a struggle for her life and even her free will against a once-trusted lover who has assured her…

You're Mine.

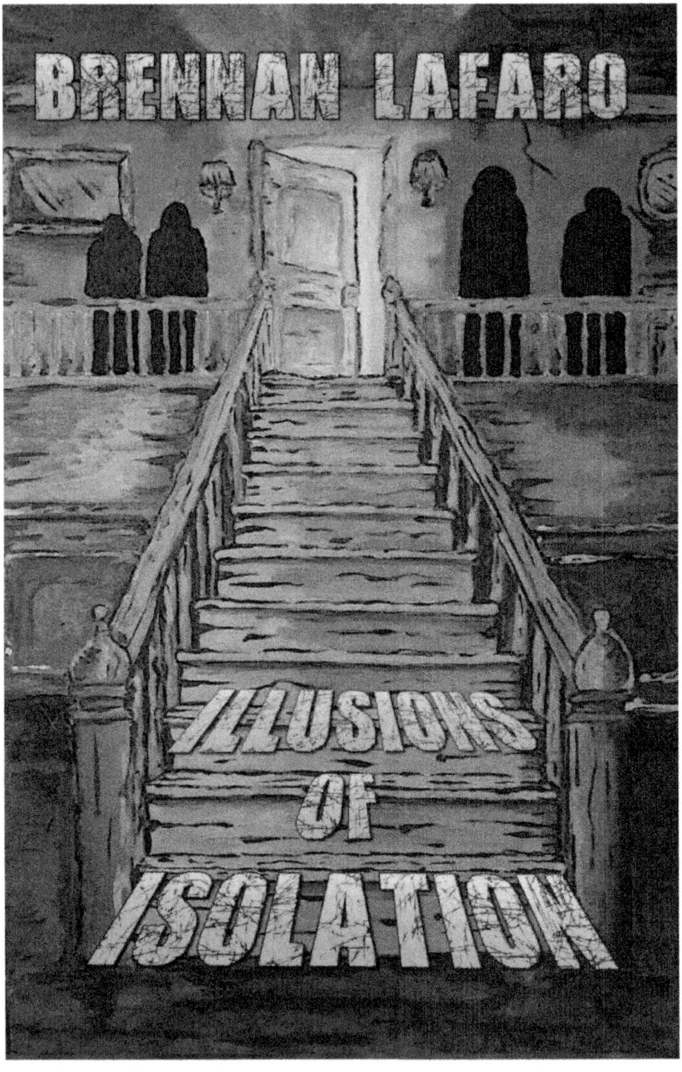
BRENNAN LAFARO
ILLUSIONS
OF
ISOLATION

Is anyone ever really alone?

When a young man's wife goes away for the weekend, he lies awake all night wondering what the otherworldly sound in the attic is and why only he can hear it.

After her husband's death, a mother who interacts with her son exclusively through. stationery notes grapples with the strange ways her lost love seems to be haunting them both.

And inch by inch, room by room, a young girl's home is overtaken by a savage jungle, even while her parents are being gradually replaced by somewhat…wilder housemates.

In this debut collection Brennan LaFaro, the author of *Noose* and *Slattery Falls*, brings you these stories of creeping dread and much, much more. Contained within are thirteen tales of horror, humor, and heart, (including nine which have never before seen the light of day) and an introduction by the legendary Jonathan Janz.

Is anyone ever really alone? Or are they merely suffering…

Illusions of Isolation?